Ex-Library: Friends of
Lake County Public Library

VOODOO SEASON

A Marie Laveau Mystery

Jewell Parker Rhodes

ATRIA BOOKS

New York London Toronto Sydney

LAKE COUNTY PUBLIC LIBRARY

3 3113 02379 9648

ATRIA BOOKS

1230 Avenue of the Americas
New York, NY 10020

This book is a work of fiction. Names, characters, places and incidents are products
of the author's imagination or are used fictitiously. Any resemblance to actual events
or locales or persons, living or dead, is entirely coincidental.

Copyright © 2005 by Jewell Parker Rhodes

All rights reserved, including the right to reproduce this book or portions thereof in
any form whatsoever. For information address Atria Books, 1230 Avenue of the
Americas, New York, NY 10020

ISBN-13: 978-0-7434-8327-8
ISBN-10:   0-7434-8327-8

First Atria Books hardcover edition August 2005

10 9 8 7 6 5 4 3 2 1

ATRIA BOOKS is a trademark of Simon & Schuster, Inc.

For information regarding special discounts for bulk purchases, please contact
Simon & Schuster Special Sales at 1-800-456-6798 or business@simonandschuster.com

Manufactured in the United States of America

Special thanks to Deborah Losse, Suzanne Pezulli,
and my editor, Malaika Adero. All wondrous women.

THE MIDDLE

Two Thousand and Five

You can't escape history or spirits singing in your blood.
When the mind refuses, the body knows.

—The Origins and History of the Voodoo Faith

She was cloaked in mist—soft as silk, cold as ice, darker than the bayou on a moonless night. "Marie." She was blind in a world without parameters, borders. Only sound. Raw feelings.

"Marie."

She couldn't breathe.

"Marie"—a dry, reedy call; then, mournful, like a keening from a wounded animal or a lost child. "Marie."

The mist grew heavy, the weight of the world was pulling her down, sucking out air, life—pulling her down into a swamp of memories:

She, just ten, watching a man writhing on the floor, a snake circling his neck; she, a woman grown, strapped to a tree, scars crisscrossing her back; she, an old woman singing, "Oh, Mary, don't you weep, don't you moan"; she, trembling, diving into thick, heady water, catfish brushing her thighs; then, a mother, screaming, giving birth, as she, the babe, slipped out, swimming downstream in a rush of water, a bloodied, blue-red membrane covering her face.

Except she was none of these. She was in her apartment, in her own bed. With a man she'd picked up at Cajun House. And she wasn't cold; she sweated from the heat of his body, from his hands stroking her breasts, his pelvis rubbing against hers.

Was she dreaming? Hallucinating?

"A haunting," her friend, Ellie, would say. "Spirits out of place. Talking." Marie didn't believe in ghosts. She was a doctor, objective. Good in a crisis.

"Marie." A soft chant.

"Marie." The mist cleared. Drums resounded and she swayed in a dress shimmering with rainbows. "Marie." Arms outstretched, flames spiraled from her fingertips. She felt herself rise. Snakes slithered across the floor. A sweet voice counterpointed the drums: "Home. Let's go home." A burst of light, a swirling of fireflies.

"Marie." Hands tugged at her skirt, pulling her down. "Heal me"; "No, heal me." Faces: black, brown, white—some staring reverently, some desperately, some enviously. Features fading: no eyes, only mouths. Wailing, screaming: "No, me. Heal me"; "Maman Marie, please. Heal me."

Fingers plucked at her skin, ripping her skirt, tugging, threatening to trample her down to the ground.

She screamed.

"Sssh," a voice murmured, a tongue licking her ear.

"Sssh," she echoed, chest heaving.

Mist pressed against her eyes, breasts, abdomen. Her back arched. Mouth open, a mist flew inside her—surrounding, squeezing her heart.

Something—someone—rocked inside her, consuming her from

the inside out. Eating her whole. "Get out. Damn you, get out."
Arms flailing, she bucked against the weight inside her. "Get
out." *Shadows flew out of her mouth.*

Marie screamed.

"Heh, you're not going crazy on me, are you? Not getting
wild, are you?"

He had a lovely smile. Skin, smooth as espresso; eyes, obsidian
black.

"You wish," she exhaled, trembling. "Get me a drink. Please."

He reached for her warm, waterlogged scotch.

"No, cold. There's beer in the fridge." She didn't watch him
go. Didn't watch his panther strut. She'd hoped he'd be a good-
enough lover so she wouldn't dream, hallucinate, or whatever
the hell her mind was doing.

She reached for her robe, catalogued her vitals—pulse elevated, breath ragged; her hands, the top of her lip, moist with
sweat. *Always the same. Same dream. Same moment of awakening.*

Marie shuddered. The dream always seemed real.

Crotch moist, she'd wanted to swallow him whole. Wanted to
be loved so well, she didn't have any weird dreams. She'd thought
about saying "no" to a condom, hoping flesh upon flesh would
banish dreams. Hauntings.

But she knew better. Knew how sperm impregnated egg, seen
cells dividing in a petri dish. Seen, too, a virus leeching on cells,
devouring them, destroying in its wake. Seen plenty of young
men, as beautiful as him, turn skeletal. Eyes sunken into bone.
Seen young women, jaws slack, transfixed by nothingness.

"Brought you a Coors. *Bien?*"

"Sure."

"Brought you a wet towel, too. Heated it up in the microwave."

"This a sushi bar?"

"*Non.* Just a little courtesy. Thought you'd like to clean your-self off."

Lord, he was good-looking. "How old are you?"

"Nineteen."

"Just a boy. You've got to go."

In the dim, smoke-filled bar, she'd missed his youth. She'd been focused on the sway of his hips, the tilt of his head. Been focused on her need to be held.

"All evening, I was man enough. Plenty, I'd say."

Untying her robe, he kissed her neck. With her best tea towel, he gently wiped her breasts, abdomen, between her thighs. "*Très belle,*" he murmured. "*Très belle.*"

She stood awkwardly, her arms dangling. He sat on the bed, his towel raised like an offering.

"You should go," she said. "I've got to get to work."

"See you?"

"Maybe." She stared at the tangled sheets. Egyptian cotton scented with semen and the boy's smell. Musty with a hint of jas-mine. Not a harsh thing about him. Just good-looking and sweet.

His pants on, she blushed, remembering how she'd kissed his lean torso, let her hands roam inside cool linen, untied his draw-string belt.

"Got any money? *Un peu?* A little?"

"Out." She held up his shoes, socks.

He winked, tucked his footwear beneath his arm and swept up his shirt from the floor. "Au'voir."

She listened for the click of the door's latch.

On the nightstand was a pack of Gauloises. She didn't smoke, but the blue package seemed as exotic as a black man speaking French.

She stepped onto her narrow balcony—wrought iron twisted into vines, leaves, a riotous garden with snakes that, depending upon the light, seemed to slither and weave from one end to the other.

Not quite dawn. Stars twinkled bravely. The skyline fanned out like a lady ready for slumber on a chaise longue. Fog rolled in from the Gulf. Later, the city would be hot, steaming. Bodies would begin swaying, stripping away clothes, ordering bourbon, another hearing of "When the Saints Go Marching In," 'til it was dusk, mosquitoes rising, and time for another nightly round of dancing, loving, dying in the city. It both fascinated and repelled her.

She felt she was back in time. No modern buildings, no high-rises. Only church spirals. Roofs with lattice trims. Gargoyles facing south. She liked the intricate warren of European-like streets. She'd been drawn to the top-floor apartment, just off the historic Quarter. Her rent was outrageous, but she liked the view, the scent of fish, beignets from the Café du Monde, the odor of alcohol, and too many bodies pressed into a too-tight space. She lit a cigarette, inhaled, and felt like the mist was inside her again. She pressed the cigarette against the rail. Sparks flew.

"Chérie?"

The boy was on the street, still barefoot, bare-chested. His shirt and shoes were tied together like a hobo sack, swinging from his hand. His feet moved—two steps forward, hips dipping, sliding side to side, and she knew he was hearing the zydeco beat. The driving staccato, the unrestrained energy. He was hearing an intense two-step as old as the cobblestone. A rhythm built on the backs of slaves.

When she'd met him, he'd said, "Dance," his hand outstretched. No, "Let's?" just a command: "Dance." She'd clutched his hand and swayed to the zydeco for hours, drank juleps, and, for a while, forgot she was a northerner down South. Forgot she was lonely. Out of her league. A battered young catfish, belly-up, flailing for air.

"It was good, wasn't it?" he called up.

"Bien. Très bien," she said, and he smiled at her like a child given candy. She should've shouted: "No, a bad dream." But she didn't want to be heartless. Too many men had accused her of that.

"Comment t'appelles-tu?"

She shook her head. "What's yours?"

"Jacques," he called up. Then, he spun around, dancing, fingers snapping, butt shaking down Rue de Christi. Without looking back, he waved. Gave an extra jerk to his behind.

Marie laughed.

Somewhere a voice caroled: "Catfish. Buy. Price fine. Come and buy."

A child, no more than ten, wandered home from tap-dancing for tourists. Pop bottle caps were a poor boy's cleats. His shoes scraped and clicked. He yawned, rubbed his eyes.

Three transvestites, legs wobbly on stiltlike heels, arms linked, wigs slightly askew, giggled. A tired sailor stepped out of a bar, his blond curls matted beneath his sailor cap. A man gripped his buttocks and they stumbled into an embrace. Then, hand outstretched, the thick-necked man guided the sailor around a corner, into an alley. Up against the wall.

"Dance," Marie whispered, rueful. "Dance."

Somewhere a sax began a lament. Church bells rang, a wild cacophony from parish churches: 6:00 A.M. Sunday. Time for all good Catholics to repent.

Marie reached for another cigarette. What the hell. She was in a foreign land. New Orleans. Just words on a map. "Gateway to the Mississippi!"—she'd been drawn like a moth to a flame. She should've gone to San Francisco. Kansas. Texas, even. Six months here and she couldn't have a climax without some will-o'wisp, some haint interfering, spoiling her body's pleasure.

Inexplicably, she started to cry. She hadn't cried since she was ten and discovered her mother dead in their attic apartment.

Furious, Marie wiped away tears.

Jacques zigzagged down the street's heart. His shirt, now loose, flapped like a sail.

She almost called out to him. What would she say? "Stop." "Don't leave." "I'm a stranger here."

Why hadn't she told him her name? Marie Levant. Yet, for most of her life, she'd been called Mary. Only one day in New Orleans, and the *r* became guttural. Plain Mary became *Marie*, spoken with the flair and accent reminiscent of her mother. "Ma–r–ie." Her mother had called her that: "Ma–r–ie. My little girl."

"Aw, Ma. Dearest Ma." She exhaled bitter smoke.

The sun crowned like a baby, spreading blood across the horizon. Blackbirds dove, screeching like their feathers were on fire.

Where was she?

"Don't you know, child? City of Sin."

She spun around. Her apartment was empty.

Yet as surely as she was alive now, breath harsh, blood rushing beneath skin, wishing she were simple enough to keep a man— to enjoy, longer than a night, the charms of a boy named Jacques—someone—*something*—chanted her name:

"Marie."

"Hey, Almost-Doctor? What's cooking?"

Marie smiled. "Not a doctor yet."

Sully, the security guard, sat on the metal folding chair, his fat legs stretched before him, turned out like a ballerina's. He'd play the harmonica, if you asked. His blunt hands moving with grace. A moan, sweet and insistent, coming from metal, his blue-black lips pinched and breathing into tiny holes. Sensual enough to quiet any Emergency Room alarm. She'd seen Sully soothe a consumptive, a kid on crack, an old woman inhaling her last breath.

Sully was the sentinel between two worlds—outside versus inside, street people who didn't know they were dying versus patients, nearly dead and some just plain dead.

She'd been "Not-Doctor" when she'd arrived at Charity Hospital six months ago. Sully's friend, a pianist with a flair for ragtime, had been accused of seducing the bartender's daughter. He'd been found behind garbage tins, stabbed seven times.

Chest, throat, face. Marie ordered a transfusion even though it was a waste. A hypodermic to his hip had the pinched-faced man flying high enough to believe he was Scott Joplin playing an invisible piano. Sully pointed his finger for her to go, then pulled the ringed, green curtains closed. No one complained about the harmonica's wail. For hours, the sound pierced metal, drowned out wounded cries, death throes, babies being born. But they complained afterward, when Sully came out, nodded to her, whispering hoarsely, "Almost-Doctor."

That was Sully's phrase for second-year residents. Marie was a babe in the woods. New. First year. Wasn't supposed to do much without a doctor's approval. But with so few doctors, everyone so deathly sick, all the residents bent rules. Tried to ease suffering. In the early days, she'd been overwhelmed, frightened she'd make a mistake. But now she did what needed to be done. More folks were always waiting; sometimes, lined up out the door.

Severs, "the-so-light-he-passed-for-white" administrator, always complained about costs. At the end of each month, he'd pass through each floor, every department, looking for waste. Complaining about paper, "unnecessarily aggressive treatments," the overuse of expensive drugs. "Be cheap, people," he'd shout. "Even the price of detergent has gone up."

Her second month, Marie confronted him. "Don't you want quality care?"

"We can't afford it if they're dying anyway."

"What about charity?"

"We give them a bed, a place to die in. That's more than many of them have."

Severs didn't exaggerate. In St. Charles, home to the famous (some said "infamous") Charity Hospital, folks were lucky to have running water, collards, and a chamber pot.

In Charity, the sick and dying flowed like tides in the bayou. The poor waited too long for treatment: A slight cough became pneumonia; a lack of insulin led to blindness, gangrene; children who stepped on a rusty nail died painfully, stricken stiff for lack of a vaccine; and wizened ladies grew frailer, malnourished on sugar and white rice.

Dope fiends, domestic abuse cases, suicides, accidents, gang wars, even the police brutality cases that never got tried, all came to Charity. The crimes of passion were the most unsettling. Otherwise gentle men—schoolteachers, accountants—or petite housewives who gave generously to the church or heavy-set waitresses who served extra portions of pie were thrown into a rage over adultery or suspected adultery. Spouses were mutilated, burned, hit with a hammer in their sleep. Even a priest shot a beloved in the confessional; then himself, through the eye. But it was the prostitutes who fared the worst; no one lamented their passing, their crippling by unnatural men. Runaways, grandmothers, perfume-scented call girls were battered, bruised, cut up, locked in a sisterhood of pain. Marie worked feverishly, trying to help as many as she could. Trying to save the lives of even those who didn't want to be saved.

Marie felt like Sisyphus, measuring her success in final minutes, giving kindness, succor to those who didn't expect any.

She even made peace with Severs. By her third month, she understood that understaffed or not, Charity provided more service to the uninsured than any other hospital in the city, perhaps the entire state. She purchased two boxes of Tide, taped red bows on them, and handed them to Severs.

He winked. "Much obliged." Then he turned around, his nasal voice blaring, "You can donate your paycheck, too."

"I was thinking I'd do that next month," she hollered at his retreating back.

"Careful," murmured Bill, a lab technician, working his fourteenth hour of a twelve-hour shift, "He'll take you up on it."

By month four, Marie finally got it—everyone on the staff gave to Charity, working more hours than they were ever paid for . . . working hard and lean. "Reuse, refresh, recycle, when you can," demanded Severs. Linens were patched and mended; days-old leftovers became soup; even gauze was cut to a perfect fit. Still, every day, the hospital struggled to provide twenty-first-century care on a nineteenth-century budget.

Marie loved it, loved beating back the odds.

* * *

Tonight, the Emergency Room was filled. Marie felt the familiar adrenaline rush. Fluorescent lights buzzed, threatening to go out. Floors were dingy. Bathrooms were worse: urine that missed the tank, vomit that didn't.

Despite DO NOT signs, people smoked. Some even drank gin out of a paper cup. The languages were amazing: Spanish, Latin, Cambodian, a Creole patois, staccato Cajun, even the drawl of a backwoods South. A multilingual world punctuated with grunts, whimpers, and moans. No suburban crises here. No fingers sliced from cutting a bagel. No broken collarbones from peewee hockey.

In Charity, Marie felt useful, alive. Nearly happy.

Her hands itched. She buttoned her resident coat, gathered her tools: stethoscope, thermometer, reflex hammer, tongue depressor, light. She loved Sunday shifts. "No rest for the Devil," her mother would say. A lapsed Catholic, Marie hoped to beat Him back. Fight Him off a few rounds.

"Had your pincushion stuck, your cork popped?"

"Ellie, hush." Ellie, "El," for short, was head nurse for the night shift. She had purple eye shadow and red nails that curved inward like a witch's. But Marie had seen El's tenderness. Seen her hold a stranger's hands for hours while he died, change an old woman's bedpan with grace.

"Well, you told me not to be blunt. Not to say 'laid.'"

"It's wrong to say anything. Haven't you any shame?"

"No." El handed her a chart. "Well, did you? Get laid?"

Marie smiled.

El cooed, "Now that's what I'm talking about. Doctor, heal thyself!"

Marie jutted her elbow into El's ever-expanding waist. "What's cooking?"

"Everything."

It was true—internal bleeding (trauma from a baseball bat), concussions, broken jaws, cancer (mainly lung), third-degree burns, and gunshot wounds. From six to six, dusk to dawn, they'd be on their feet. El could've assigned another nurse to her but most times stayed close to Marie. They made a good team.

Once Marie had asked boldly about El's love life.

"Child, I'm sixty-eight. Been married five times. Got me a cat. A snake. A dog. That's all I need. I'm living vicariously through you."

Marie'd been shocked. Not by the lack of sex, but by El's agelessness. Skin unlined, fresh like a girl's. Maybe it was the humidity?

"Magnolia blossoms."

"What?"

"My beauty secret. Magnolias."

Marie just shook her head and went back to stitching a hand that had been caught in a steel fishing net.

Marie and El never left the first floor. They sent patients upstairs, never to be seen again, or downstairs to the morgue. When they were lucky, they got to send a few home.

By 2:00 A.M., the Emergency Room had quieted some. Huan, a Vietnamese from California, was laying out bandages and alcohol swipes; K-Paul, a local boy and the best diagnostician, slept, softly snoring; and Pretty Meredith, who only had to look at her patients for them to quiet, awestruck by her blonde-haired, blue-eyed, Minnesotan beauty, was meticulously filling out paperwork. Then, herself: Marie, average height, more lean than voluptuous. Her hair, thick, wavy, and black, was her crowning glory but she kept it confined in a careless ponytail. She wanted to sleep, to dream about Jacques. The supervising doctor, Pierre DuLac, was already drunk in his office, weeping into a shot glass. Everybody said he desired to be a *houngan*, a voodoo priest, but he lacked the gift. Being a doctor was second best. Technicians, nurses, even other doctors told her this in all seriousness. As if

DuLac were a tragic figure, a would-be saint. No one reported him to the oversight board. Everyone was waiting for his redemption.

She'd been warned: "Crazy folks down South." And they were. But somehow she felt at home with these folks. Inside the hospital, she felt safe.

K-Paul woke, shouting, "Shit's hit the fan."

Persistent whines, like cats being neutered, kept spiraling, drawing closer. Even DuLac stumbled out of his office. Three? Four? Maybe five ambulances? None of them sent uptown.

"Here," "Over here," medics were shouting, slamming through the swinging doors. "Bust-up at Breezy's."

"What's that?" asked Huan.

"An old slave shack turned into an illicit bar," answered DuLac. "Brew isn't bad."

"You should know," scowled Marie.

Meredith coughed.

K-Paul whispered, "Way to go."

"Let's go to work," hollered El.

"I'm sorry," said Marie. But DuLac had already moved on.

El and her nurses began sorting the seriously injured from the less so.

"Assault rifles. Some gang shit," a medic said, awed, as if everyone didn't already know. Blood dripped like Kool-Aid.

But it was El who noticed the give in the medic's knees, the unfocused gaze, the weary, hangdog face.

"You're in shock. Sit down. Head between your knees."

Many had multiple wounds—some dead; some dying; some

sent upstairs to die on the operating table. Marie's mantra: "Don't get emotional." Check pulses, plug holes, stitch, add hemoglobin. But she still cried when they died. Just seemed there ought to be more healing in her hands.

Just as it seemed she ought to have been able to stop her mother from dying. She swayed, nauseous. *Mother?*

"This one's for the morgue," said George, one of the ambulance crew.

The shrouded body was small, almost dwarfed by the gurney. A hand dangled, forlorn and exposed.

"Wait." Marie pressed her fingers to the frail wrist. No pulse. The ribcage didn't move.

"Go ahead. The morgue."

She smelled honeysuckle. Her mother's scent.

"Wait."

"Dead is dead," said the paramedic.

"Did you do CPR?" Marie knew it was hopeless. Too much time without a pulse. She caught up the hand again. Odd, it was still soft, warm.

"What is it, Marie?" DuLac asked, applying pressure to a chest wound, a gaping hole in a young man's side. The man was trying to speak; red foam bubbled out of his mouth.

"What is it?"

No stains, Marie thought. No blood. The sheet was pristine.

"Marie, what is it?"

"I don't know." The ER was chaos—noisy panic; crying, whimpering; doctors shouting, a man gasping, wailing like an infant. She was needed elsewhere. Still, she couldn't move.

She heard singing. A nursery song. Words too quiet to understand.

"Take the body to the morgue." El was beside her.

George nodded, slipping on his headsets, blaring Queen Ida singing, "Bad Moon Rising."

"No, wait."

"It's done. Over with," El said bluntly.

Marie looked across at DuLac. His fingertips were closing the dead man's eyes.

"DuLac," she whispered, not knowing why. He looked up, startled.

Marie lifted the sheet. She sucked in air. *An angry, red mark was on the girl's forehead.*

The girl was beautiful. Sixteen, maybe. Skin, pale; lashes, golden-tipped and damp. Like she'd been crying before she died.

Quickly, Marie checked again for life. Pulse. Heart. Her hands roamed the girl's limbs, her breasts.

"My God." She took El's hand and laid it on the girl's abdomen. The protrusion wasn't great, but it was there. Hard. Something curled inside.

"C-section," DuLac yelled. He peered at the mark. "Fast."

"Call upstairs," said El.

"No time. Doc Marie," DuLac rolled the *r* in the back of his throat. "*Sainte Marie* will do it."

"Are you crazy?"

"*Non.*" DuLac held out his hands. A slight tremor. "I'm not fit. The babe will die before it reaches the operating room."

Marie nodded. "Huan, help me." The Vietnamese girl was at her side with a tray of surgical instruments. Marie mouthed "Thanks." In seconds, she and El backed the gurney into a station. El closed the curtains. "She looks like a bride," breathed Huan, before cutting into satin, exposing the girl's abdomen.

Marie sliced deep, yet not too deep. There was the babe, fist-sized, barely alive. A blue-red membrane covered her face.

"Cut it off. Now. Cut it off." DuLac scared her. Where'd he come from? Marie sliced at the membrane; it was fibrous, thick, slippery with blood. Tiny lungs were barely expanding. Frantic, Marie tore the covering from the child's head.

"A caul," said El.

"Evil," said Huan.

"The gift of sight," answered DuLac.

The babe was gulping air. *"Sssh. Mon piti bébé. Fais dodo,"* Marie crooned, her finger clearing mucus from the baby's mouth.

"When did you learn patois?"

"What are you talking about?"

"Leave her be, El. She has a baby to see to."

El looked from DuLac to Marie. "Huan, do you mind calling upstairs? Tell them we need a crib in intensive care."

"I think she'll be fine," said Marie, counting fingers and toes. She leaned toward the mother. The child was tinged brown, so either the mother was a Creole, a mixed blood, or the father was black. Marie held the squalling baby near her mother's face. "She's beautiful. Like you. Very beautiful."

The dead woman's hand clutched Marie's elbow.

"Reflex," said El.

"Just passing over," said DuLac.

"You're both crazy," answered Marie, trembling, ashamed of her fear.

"Didn't your mother teach you anything?"

"What do you mean?"

DuLac shrugged. "El, take care of things."

"Sure," El said, more submissive than Marie had ever heard her.

"I'll check on the others."

"Not get a drink?" As soon as she said it, Marie felt ashamed.

DuLac placed his palm on the baby's head, murmuring, "She's going to be fine. Remarkable, *Sainte Marie*."

"Stop calling me that."

"*Sainte*. Doctor. Physician. Mary Levant—isn't that what your foster parents called you? What's in a name?"

"Stay out of my business, DuLac."

"Doctor, if you please." Then, he smiled gleefully, clapped his hands, "You saw what no one else did. I think you will again."

Marie was confused. She didn't know why she was rude to DuLac. Oddly enough she sensed he liked her. That he was testing her. Telling her something he felt she needed to know.

The curtains swayed shut.

Marie turned her attention to the baby, cleaning its skin with a towel. She avoided the mother's limp legs, the split-open abdomen.

El smoothed the dead girl's hair. Covered her body with a blanket. Still the blood seeped through.

Without looking at Marie, El said, "DuLac did the surgery. Not you. You'd both be in a world of trouble." She lifted the caul from the tray, wrapped it in a towel.

"What're you doing?"

"Need to bury it."

"Why?"

"Didn't your mother teach you anything?" It was the same question DuLac had asked.

Marie closed her eyes. *She could almost hear her mother, telling her to hide: "Shadows be good. Good for staying safe." Then, her mother murmuring into her ear: "You're special, don't let anyone tell you different." Almost as though her mother knew she was going to die.*

"Pray to the Virgin," her mother told her over and over. "Be a good Catholic." But Marie knew she'd never been baptized. When pressed, her mother snapped angrily, "You don't need another blessing."

Marie opened her eyes. El was staring at her. Marie answered flatly: "I told you my mother died when I was ten."

"Mmm," clucked El. "But not before she taught you Creole. How do you explain that? Miss North? Chicago? Or wherever it is you claim you from?"

"El, you don't understand." Marie felt hurt, deep and unfathomable. The baby started crying, her head and mouth searching for Marie's breast. "I'll take her upstairs."

"You do that."

"El, please, don't be mad at me." Marie felt she was a child again, living with foster parents, trying to keep the peace, promising to be good.

"You don't know, do you?"

"Know what?" Her voice was a lament.

El smiled. "Never mind. Take the baby upstairs. Let her suck your thumb. It'll keep her satisfied for a while."

Marie smiled, feeling the world was all right again. She held the baby close, singing, *"Mon piti bébé, mon piti bébé. La lune toute jaune, se lève."* All the flurry of activity fell away. No bodies, no voices urgent and panicked. No odor of death. Only the smell of fresh leaves and honeysuckle as she held the baby close, crooning over the perfectly formed face.

El swung open the curtains. "Medic," she yelled, swift and sharp. "Morgue."

She watched Marie enter the elevator like a proud mother. Then, she crossed to DuLac, stitching an unconscious man's leg in the corridor.

"Your hands seem fine to me."

DuLac shrugged.

"You know whose girl that be? The one who died."

"Oui," sighed DuLac. "Trouble on the way."

"I'll call her mother."

"Her mother knows."

El touched a nail to her cheek. "You think she'll come?"

"Non. Not to bury the daughter."

"Or claim a grandchild?"

"That I don't know."

"You mean you don't know or you can't see?"

"I can't see." He tied off the suture. "When the time comes, she will."

"Our Marie?"

"Oui. She's got a mouth on her."

El laughed, then gulped, swallowing a cry. "But is her heart big enough?"

DuLac stood, towering over the tough Miss El. He caressed her cheek. *"Que penses-tu?* What you think?"

El inhaled. She looked back at the small, blanketed body on the gurney. "That was one pretty girl."

"Dammit to hell. Someone get this body out of here. Get it out of my sight."

THE BEGINNING

Two Thousand and Five

How was I to know they were all in my blood?
Seven generations. All of them—whispering, punishing,
crying to get out.

—Marie's journal, February 2005

Marie could recall a time when it felt good to be held, rocked—daytime, nighttime, "all around the town time" in her mother's honeysuckle arms. No one else had had the sweet scent. She didn't recognize it until she came to New Orleans. Where did her mother ever get it? Honeysuckle during Chicago winters? Year after year? In and out of season?

In the South, honeysuckle bloomed year-round. The scent was cloying, overwhelming. Even the bees seemed irritated by the smell.

But this newborn baby smelled like the flower. Delicate. Like her mother.

Sometimes Marie had felt their roles were reversed: she, the grown-up; her mother, the child. Sweet, withdrawn, her mother often seemed in another world. Humming off-key in a distant place where it never snowed, money wasn't needed, and where she didn't clean houses, collect bottles for pennies, and didn't sew or patch their clothes.

When Marie hurt most, when school kids taunted her about her worn shoes, ketchup sandwiches, and her crazy, muttering mother, it was the memory of her mother's sweet aroma that calmed her.

Saturdays, when her mother went to St. Teresa's Retirement Home to wipe tired bodies, change bedpans, sheets, and listen to old nun's stories, Marie would lie in her mother's bed, inhaling her warm scent, whiling away the hours pretending her mother was home, rich enough to put her feet up and be bored on a Saturday.

Her mother said she went to St. Teresa's for penance, but, afterward, she was always pleased when the nuns gave her beans, rice, a can of Spam. They'd have a feast on Sunday. Her mother, stirring red beans, smelling of honeysuckle; she, Marie, reading a book, and they'd pretend they were safe, secure, and happy.

The moment Marie walked into pediatric intensive care, she could pick out the scent. She wondered if anybody else could. During breaks, after work, before work, she stared into the baby's bright, glassy eyes. Inhaling the aroma, she thought she was drowning, seeing her mother's face.

Marie went to Maison Blanche, the city's finest department store. They had myriad perfumes blended with flowers, chemicals, and oils, but none of them, pure honeysuckle.

At night when policemen were riding stallions at the other end of the park, Marie plucked honeysuckle from vines where it grew wild, untamable. Sometimes it shivered in the night air, and Marie felt the blooms were alive, offering themselves to her.

Using an old pharmacist's pestle, she ground the flowers until they yielded droplets of heaven.

Marie dabbed honeysuckle behind her ears, along her cleavage. She felt comforted—even though her dreams hadn't lessened, even though each morning, she woke in a sweat, on the verge of screaming.

She wanted to confide in El, to tell her about her strange dreams, about the baby's sweet scent.

But El always warned, "It ain't your baby."

Marie couldn't help the hours spent holding the motherless child. Before shifts, during breaks, after work.

Each day, the infant was getting stronger. Each day, she became more attached, afraid to let go.

"What's going to happen to her?" she asked Antoinette, the social services director.

"Foster care."

Marie knew what foster care could be like. Indifferent, at best; cruel, at worst. But she imagined someone would rescue the child. The dead mother's people. They'd sweep in, declaring, "That's our child. Our family."

But sometimes, just sometimes, late, when she'd awakened from her dream, after she'd fed the baby Similac (when her womb strangely ached, when her lips feathered the baby's brow with kisses), the thought would hover, echo through her consciousness—*the child could be hers.*

Another black single mother—how stereotypical.

She didn't have time for a child. Still, she was tempted.

Even the baby seemed to know her. Four pounds, six ounces, at birth, the baby wouldn't feed. A tiny pink tongue spat out the latex nipple. Only Marie could encourage her to start taking a bottle. To suck rather than be fed intravenously. Now six pounds, two ounces, Marie was proud of the baby's small mound of a belly.

Sometimes the baby cried, wailed like she was dying, pained by some hidden wound. Nobody else could calm her.

Marie was the baby's medicine.

Something wonderful, magical happened between them. For hours, the child watched her; she watched the child as if no one else in the world existed.

Mon piti bébé. Fais dodo, mon piti bébé.

The baby's lids would struggle to stay open. But, always, the lilting tune lulled the baby to sleep. The child would go limp like a rag doll. It was startling how the child would go from bright, red rage, fists balled and tears raining down her face, to utter calm. The first couple of times, Marie panicked and unbundled the blanket, unsnapped the undershirt to make certain the lungs were expanding, the chest rising and falling.

Mon piti bébé. Fais dodo. Mon piti bébé.
My little baby. Go to sleep. My little baby.

Except it wasn't accurate French. It should've been *Ma petite*. "Go to sleep" should've been "Endors-toi." It was Creole. How'd she learn it?

She couldn't remember. She just knew the song. Knew all its verses:

Fais dodo, mon piti bébé.
La lune toute jaune, se lève.
Fais dodo, mon piti bébé.

Quand tu rêveras, rêve des esprits
qui survolent la mer.
Fais dodo, mon piti bébé.

Quand tu te réveilleras, seize ans tu auras.
Réveille-toi mort.
Fais dodo, mon piti bébé, mon piti si doux.
Fais dodo!

It always worked. When she'd tried the song in English:

Sssh, my little baby. Go to sleep, my little baby.
The moon is yellow, rising high.
Little baby, go to sleep.

When you dream, dream of spirits
flying across the sea.
My little baby, sleep.

When you wake, sixteen you'll be.
Wake yourself from the dead.
Go to sleep, little baby, my pretty baby.
Sleep!

It never worked. The baby cried and cried, gasping for air.

* * *

"We'll be moving her to the nursery tomorrow."

Marie shuddered. "Has anyone come to claim her?"

Antoinette shook her head. "Two weeks, not a word. Not even an ID on the mother."

Marie buried her nose against the baby's cheek. She stroked the fragile fingers, the tiny nails.

"You could name her, you know?" Antoinette dressed like a banker instead of a social worker. Silk suits with clean lines.

"Doesn't seem right."

"Why? Are you afraid of keeping her?"

"No. Afraid of letting her go."

Marie laid the baby in the bassinet. "Don't worry. I'll find your people." She kissed the child's brow.

The elevator slid smoothly down.

"You didn't name her yet, did you?" El didn't look up from the papers at her station. Marie noticed her nails were blue this week.

"What can I help with?" Marie put on her white coat, a stethoscope dangling from her pocket. "Pneumonia? Fever? Vision impairment? Ears going deaf?"

"Don't name her. If you do, you won't let her go."

"I liked it better when you were asking about my love life."

"So did I. You got one?"

Marie laughed. "No." Then she leaned over the counter, embracing El.

Flustered, El pushed her away.

Marie smiled. "Put me to work, El. Otherwise, I'll hug you again."

"Sass. Nothing but sass. Red peppers in you."

"And not in you?"

El slapped a clipboard on the counter. It held a pencil and a blank sheet.

"I got an odd one for you. DuLac wants you to help him with a patient. 'Course the boy's dead, but he said he needed your help."

"What does he think I can do?"

"Lord knows. But do I ask the almighty doctor? Last time I checked, he was still the boss."

"Right. I'm going."

"Good. Last urgent care room."

"That's unusual for a dead man."

"You bet. Taking up my space," El grumbled. "Stop by later," she called after Marie. "I've got a rattle for the baby."

Marie stopped at the door. Through the glass, she knew someone was sitting in the corner. Smoke spiraled upward, hovering in a thin layer on the ceiling.

"Smoking's not allowed. Bad for the patients."

"I didn't think it much mattered to him."

Marie was glad her hand was still on the door; it steadied her. *She felt—what? Recognition? Déjà vu?*

He was average height like her. More interesting than handsome. Arched brows. High cheekbones like a Choctaw's. Lashes so long, they touched his cheeks when he blinked. His hair was jet black, pulled tight in a ponytail. He was dressed in black shirt, black pants, a leather bomber jacket, and wore a gold cross dangling in his left ear.

Marie exhaled. She realized she'd been holding herself incredibly still because he'd been still. Like a stop-motion character. Paused. Expectant.

He pinched off the cigarette. Ash was on his index finger and thumb. "If you say I'm as still as an Indian, I'll have to arrest you."

He drawled. Marie grinned.

"You know everybody in Louisiana mixed with something. I'm just a good old southern boy."

"Like hell."

"Nice to meet you, too."

Marie shook his hand. "Doctor Levant."

"Reneaux."

She raised her brow.

"Frenchmen used to own my family. I'm plain southern, through and through. Work for the New Orleans Police Department."

"Undercover?"

"Naw. Just a detective."

"No uniform? Not even a suit?"

"Even nuns have given up the habit. Don't you get tired of that white coat?"

"Very funny."

DuLac swept in, snapping his gloves on. Marie flinched at the sound.

"You two been getting to know one another? *Bon.* Reneaux is an old friend. He wanted us to take a look at this one—since it's the second we've found."

"The second what?" asked Marie.

"Murder."

"Death for no apparent cause," added Reneaux.

"You were the first to notice something odd about the girl. I wanted you to take a look at this, too."

"I don't know what you're talking about."

Marie could see the girl's body stretched, languid, petal-open, just before she sliced into the abdomen. Smooth, soft skin, free of bruises, wounds . . . a body that seemed not to have died.

"The baby's mother," insisted DuLac.

DuLac drew close, too close. Marie could see the pores in his skin, the redness of his eyes. She smelled licorice trying to mask alcohol.

"Two bodies that shouldn't have died. Both marked with some sign. A mystery, don't you think?"

"I'm just a doctor."

"I think you see more than you let on. Humor me." DuLac swept off the sheet, it rose, buoyant and, for a second, Marie saw the barest outline of a body. Then, the sheet, as if swept up by an ill wind, went awry, settling on the floor.

"My Lord."

Both men looked at her. She closed her eyes, then forced herself to open them.

"You knew him?" asked Reneaux.

"Yes. His name is—"

"—was," corrected Reneaux.

"—Jacques."

Marie bit the inside of her lip, tasting blood. "Don't get emotional," she murmured.

Jacques's forehead was marked like the girl's. Even in death, his body was beautiful.

Flashes of memory: her, holding him, kissing him—there and there; feeling his teeth biting her breast; his body inside hers.

Lord, she mustn't blush. It was a body. Fluids, flesh, sinews, cartilage, organs. An impersonal body. "The spirit has passed," as DuLac would say.

It looked as if Jacques hadn't died in pain. She brushed his hair back from his brow.

"Some kind of chalk. Powder. Odd," she murmured. "A cross? Upside down?"

The men looked at each other.

She lifted his arms. No needle marks. She felt his abdomen. All in place. His penis and scrotum were slack. No bruises on his legs. No trauma of any kind.

"Help me turn him over."

She and DuLac wrestled the body. It was stiff and smacked awkwardly. The bridge of Jacques's nose pressed into cold metal. Marie turned his head on the side. She could almost pretend he was sunbathing. That the bright lights overhead were UV lamps.

"You knew Jacques?"

"Yes."

"How long? Where'd you meet?"

Marie cocked her head. "Are you interrogating me?"

Reneaux shrugged, palms open. "That's what detectives do."

"We went out once, that's all."

"I see." His voice pitched higher.

Marie scowled. "We'll need a toxicology report."

"I think it'll be negative," said Reneaux.

"Why?"

"This isn't the second, it's the third. A girl was found dead by the pier three weeks ago. Young. Her face marked. The coroner couldn't determine a cause of death."

"Look at him again, Marie," pleaded DuLac. "Is there anything else you see? Anything you feel?"

"You can see him as well as I can."

"No," said DuLac, longingly, his voice hoarse, "I can't."

Marie looked again.

Jacques opened his eyes.

She screamed.

*   *   *

"Reflex like hell," she thought.

"You all right?" Reneaux squatted over her, blocking her sight.

"I fainted."

"Sure did." He stood, extending a hand.

Marie shaded her eyes. The light was too bright. "You've got a halo."

"Do I?"

She was on her feet.

"Now my mama would laugh to hear that."

"Do you always drawl?"

"Do you always faint?"

"I'm sorry."

"Naw. Lash out all you want. That way you won't cry."

Marie wanted to slap him. But it was true. She did want to cry. She wanted to go upstairs, see the baby and smell honeysuckle.

"Let me take you outside. Away from the body." His voice was less drawn out, more clipped, a bass rather than a breathy tenor. "I always like playing with you Yankees. Think none of us ever

41

went to college. A southern twang means we're dumb." All the while, his elbow under her arm, he was moving Marie up, outside, toward a chair in the hall. "But a southern drawl is a birthright.

"Now Creoles think they're sophisticated 'cause they speak smatterings of French. Cajuns think they're just authentic; though, most times, nobody can understand them. But real New Orleanians are just southerners. Grits. Corn pone. Fatback. You know the stuff." He eased her down into the chair. "All those stereotypes northerners have. And if I just keep talking, you'll stay mad at me and forget you fainted and how embarrassed you feel." He filled a paper cone from the water cooler. "Here."

"You're good. You should've been a doctor."

"Some say I am. I've got a great bedside manner. You like to try?"

Laughing, Marie rocked forward. The water spilled.

Reneaux took a kerchief from his pocket, squatted again, and wiped the floor.

"Boy Scout, too."

"You betcha, ma'am." He tapped her knee. "In all seriousness, you feeling better?"

"Yes. Thank you."

"What happened?"

No more nonsense. This was the detective speaking. Forthright. Face expressionless; brown eyes piercing. Marie felt as if he could see straight through her. *She felt, too, that she knew these eyes, knew this man bent before her. Knew he had a good heart. Knew, too, that their fates were linked.*

She cupped his face in her hands. Reneaux didn't move, just kept his eyes steady on her. *She saw herself reflected—no, more than that—she saw herself inside his eyes.*

She pulled back. "I don't know what's the matter with me. Strange dreams. Strange—"

She paused, folding her hands in her lap. "I just got scared."

"I understand."

She cocked her head. "Did DuLac order the toxicology report?"

"I don't know. He just left. Thought you'd be madder than hell 'cause he saw you faint."

"He's right." She went back inside the room. "I haven't eaten."

"Been working too hard."

She squinted at Reneaux. "Not sleeping."

"You're not the type of women who usually faints."

"Never."

"'Til now." Reneaux snapped his fingers. "Dog, I didn't mean to say that."

"'Dog?' What kind of detective talk is that? You should at least say, 'damn.'"

She stopped short. Tears welled. Jacques dead. Here she was teasing, flirting.

"I'm sorry. It's hard losing someone you know."

Marie picked up the sheet and covered Jacques's torso. "The dead should have some dignity."

"The living, too? I see why DuLac thinks you can help. You have the sight."

"What're you talking about?"

Reneaux smiled, opened a small notebook. "This is what I know. Three unexplained deaths. Two women. One man. All under twenty-one."

"Jacques was nineteen."

Reneaux scribbled on his pad. "One woman. The girl, the one who was pregnant? Did you know how old she was?"

Marie shook her head. "Sixteen at most."

He scribbled more. "The deaths all took place within the city limits. A pier. An alley."

"Was that Jacques? Found in an alley?"

"Yes."

"Clothed?" She had to ask.

He shook his head. "Like you see him. Where'd they find the girl?"

"Breezy's, I think. But I don't see how this has anything to do with me. I doctor the sick, not the dead."

"Maybe you'll see some clue, sense something that will help. I trust DuLac. He knows these things."

DuLac appeared, framed in the doorway.

"Speak of the Almighty," Marie said, sarcastic. "There's nothing else I can do here, DuLac. I don't know anything."

"But you do. Give it time. You'll discover you know a great deal. About the past. The future."

"Oh, I get it," she said, jokingly. "You mean you're talking as DuLac, the would-be *houngan?* The would-be voodoo priest?"

"He's quite famous in the Quarter. Roots, herb doctor. One of the best."

"You're serious?" She looked back and forth between the two men. "This is where I'm supposed to say 'I believe.' In voodoo? Hex signs? Well, I don't."

"Marie, please."

"Doctor to you, Reneaux. Doctor Levant."

"How do you explain the baby?"

"Luck." Marie knew she often noticed things other people didn't—she was smart, intuitive. But that didn't mean she had sight. Special knowledge.

"If I could help, Reneaux, I would."

She tried to pass by DuLac.

He clutched her shoulder. "I worry if you leave, you won't accept who you are."

She looked distastefully at DuLac. He removed his hand from her shoulder.

"What made you faint?" asked Reneaux. "You saw something, Marie. I know you did."

"Sure. I saw a dead man opening his eyes. You saw it, Detective. And you." She turned back to DuLac. "The reflex startled me."

Neither man spoke.

"Look at him. A reflex. His eyes opened. It startled me. Look at him."

DuLac didn't glance away from her.

"Look," she shouted.

"You look."

Mist spiraled overhead.

"That's curious." Then Marie giggled, for she sounded like Alice talking to the Cheshire cat.

"What's curious?" asked DuLac.

Honeysuckle. She smelled it. Odd, the baby was upstairs; her mother, buried in a pauper's grave.

"Look," DuLac repeated.

She walked toward the scent, slowly, deliberately, until she was beneath the lamps—her gaze slowly, steadily, moving upward from Jacques's toes to his face.

45

His eyes were closed tight.

DuLac, his breath warm, whispered in her ear. "A reflex might open his eyes, but not close them again."

"They opened. I tell you they opened."

"I believe you. But only you saw."

"Reneaux?" Marie reached back her hand as if he could comfort her.

"I didn't see anything."

"But you did, Marie. You're the one with the gift."

"You're trying to tell me I see ghosts? You're a drunk, DuLac."

"So I am." His shoulders rounded, his chest caved inward; he seemed smaller, less powerful.

"I'm sorry." She squeezed his hand.

"I am what I am. An aging drunk. Merely competent as a doctor. But you're different, Marie. I knew it when you first stepped inside Charity. I felt it."

She felt sorry for DuLac. "I can't see ghosts."

"Spirits," he murmured.

"I'm a scientist. Objective. Twenty-eight. A woman grown. Not some young, inexperienced girl to be awed by crazy tales." *Not like Jacques.* Marie shivered. Why'd she think that?

She could see Jacques in a back room, lying on a mattress on the floor, spine curved, knees up, clasping his abdomen. There was a small altar with the Virgin and two candles. A red leather prayer book.

"He didn't die in the alley."

"How do you know?"

Marie couldn't answer.

"Ah, Chérie," *she heard.* "Chérie." *Jacques was sitting, cross-legged, eyes open.* "Dance," *he demanded, palm outstretched.*

46

"Dance."

She reached for his hand.

"You *see* something," whispered DuLac.

Marie stumbled backward. She didn't want to dance with Jacques. The dead should stay dead. It was just another outrageous dream. She was in a hospital. She treated people. Living people.

"I have to get back to work."

"What did you see, Doctor Levant?"

"Nothing."

DuLac called, adamant, "When Legba knocks, you have to open."

She kept walking.

"Hey, Doc, I'll stop by and talk to you another time."

"Good luck searching for clues, Reneaux. Sorry I couldn't help."

She wanted to run. But she made herself walk. "Don't get emotional."

One step. Then another step. Out the door. Into the ER. Into the world of flesh.

She heard Jacques calling, "Comment t'appelles-tu? T'appelles-tu?"

"Je suis Marie," *another voice answered.*

She was running full out.

"Marie!" El shouted.

Past Sully, Meredith, the admissions desk. Past all the sick, aching people. She had to get out.

She pressed the elevator buttons. One carriage on the sixth floor; the other, the ninth.

She opened the fire exit and started climbing the stairs. Seven flights to reach the baby.

Seven flights to reach home.

Legba is like St. Peter. He opens the spirit gates.

—The Origins and History of the Voodoo Faith

They'd stolen her baby.

Marie had gone to see the baby and the bassinet was empty. She'd panicked, and for a horrifying second, she'd thought the baby had died. But the two nursery nurses were watching her. Pitying her. She stalked out, just as they'd begun whispering.

Nothing in her life was calm; everything was disrupted, confused. DuLac always seemed to be watching her. El didn't even fuss; instead, she treated Marie with deference. Like she was special when she wasn't. She wanted to scream at everyone: "I'm just like you."

Jacques was dead. She hadn't seen anything. No rising from the dead, no opening of glazed eyes.

She wanted the sidelong glances, the gossip, to stop. For Sully to stop calling her "Doctor." For Huan to share her spicy noodles again. Not to be afraid of her. And for K-Paul to stop asking for her opinion. Second-guessing his diagnosis.

In the past two days, Marie had been even more desperate for the baby. Cradling her, she'd felt normal. Capable of love. Of being loved.

She didn't know she'd been fattening the baby like a lamb to the slaughter.

Instead of honeysuckle, she smelled rubbing alcohol, plastic, and gauze. The bitter odor of spent bandages, sick flesh, and Pine-Sol.

"Why didn't you warn me?"

"Because you'd throw a worse fit than you're throwing now."

"She was my baby."

"No. She was—*is*—a ward of the state."

Antoinette was wearing blue. A vase of lilies was on her desk. There was also a photo of a little girl with freckles on her nose and a smile sparkling with braces.

"Is that your daughter?"

"*Oui.* Denise."

"Would you give her up?"

"No."

"Then you understand how I feel."

Antoinette answered gently, "But she's not flesh of your flesh."

Marie felt stricken. Felt as though her womb contracted. Why did she feel the baby was her child? Was she being selfish? No husband on the horizon? Clinging to a child as her eggs aged, her biological clock ticking away?

"Baby Doe belongs in foster care."

"She belongs with me," she said softly, emphatically, certain in her bones.

"They've found her a good home, Marie. She'll be well cared for."

"Can you guarantee it? Swear it?"

"I've placed her with good people. Experienced foster parents."

"You don't understand, Antoinette. There's no such thing as good foster care."

You're always beholding, always growing up with love removed. She'd had three foster parents in eight years. All of them drumming into her that she was below average, nothing special.

The first families she'd only been with for several days. She'd run away from them both. The Duncan kids thought she was a punching bag; bruises flowered all over her body and face. The second home, Mr. Jackson liked touching her in bed, his hand clamped over her mouth. She'd gotten tired of running. Tired of complaining of abuse. Plus, she'd been warned. Institutions were perfect for rebellious, dissatisfied kids. The Harrises, she thought, were the lesser evil. She was wrong.

She could still see Mrs. Harris, flesh hanging from her arms, spooning mashed potatoes onto her plate. "Don't think you're better than anyone else. Your mother's dead. Nobody knows your father. You're lucky I feed you." She was only ten. Mrs. Harris, a good Christian, begrudged her everything. Eight long years. She didn't beat Marie, just battered her spirit. "Mary is a good, plain, Christian name. Mary you are in this house. Marie sounds like a whore."

Marie blinked.

"Please, tell me where the baby is. I need to make sure she's all right."

"I can't do that."

"What if I wanted to adopt her?"

"You'd have to prove abandonment."

"Her mother's dead. Not a soul has visited her in two months. How abandoned does she have to be?"

"Legally? At least a year. It's a judge's discretion."

Marie wanted to rage, shred Antoinette's double-breasted suit.

"I thought you were my friend, Antoinette."

"Marie, I'd love for you to raise that baby. You'd both be good for each other. You just need to be patient."

Marie turned to stalk out.

"Giving up so easily?"

Heart racing, Marie spun back around. "What do you mean?"

"I expected you to torture me."

"I thought about it."

Antoinette laughed. "Reneaux identified the mother."

"When?"

"Yesterday. Apparently, DuLac knew her."

"El, too?" Marie felt sick.

"Yes. They both know the baby's people."

Marie felt betrayed.

"If the family renounces their claim, you can adopt sooner."

"Who are they?"

"I'm not supposed to tell you. They're bayou people. Back country. They don't have a phone. I drove to see them this morning. They set their dogs on me."

"What's their name?"

"You've got to promise not to try to see them by yourself. Get a lawyer. Take a friend with you."

"What's their name?"

"I'm serious, Marie. I'm only telling you because I heard about you and that body. Everybody knows you see things."

"I don't see anything."

"You'll have to if you're going to deal with these people." Antoinette wrote four lines on a piece of paper. "Here. If anyone asks, I didn't tell you."

"Thanks, Antoinette."

"I'm not certain I'm doing you a favor."

* * *

"I'm leaving, El."

"Your shift?"

"It's an emergency. I've got to go." Marie had her purse, keys. It was at least an hour's drive, outside the city. But she had to stop, face El across the desk. "You should've told me."

She watched El age. Watched her spirit drain until she could clearly see the old woman with a bouffant wig, loud shadow, and polish. "You should've told me."

Marie hurried. She needed to save the baby.

El picked up the receiver and dialed. "She knows, DuLac. Not everything. But enough. She's on her way to the DeLaCroix house." Then she pressed the button to disconnect.

* * *

Marie had been driving for two hours. She hadn't counted on bad roads. Getting lost. But the farther she drove, the wilder the landscape became. On either side of her were willows, gnarled and ancient; thick moss hanging in sheets; and swamp, sluggish with undergrowth, rocks, and bones. Sometimes she heard the caw-cawing of birds, the violent splash of crocodile catching prey; the rustling of an animal running through bush. She turned left off the highway. Onto a packed dirt road, elevated from the swamp with tons of raw earth, sand, and wooden ties.

The note Antoinette had given her said:

DeLaCroix
Bayou Teché
Twelve miles off Route 5
Left at Junction 28

An animal appeared in front of her headlights and froze. She slammed on her brakes. She thought she'd hit it. She turned off her engine, got out of her car. Blood was on the grille. She felt heartsick.

She stepped over the wooded tie, trying to follow the animal's path. It couldn't have gotten far. The earth caved and she slid, bruising and dirtying her left side.

"Damn." She brushed at the dirt, then held her breath, listening. No whimper. No whine or moan. Just a high-pitched shriek. A splash of water. Instinctively, she moved to the right.

The setting sun, the damp, heavy thicket made progress hard. Mosquitoes were drawing blood. Her feet were sinking in mud. She stumbled, falling onto her hands and knees. Tree limbs tangled in her hair.

She should turn back. It was unsafe. She'd get lost and no one would find her. *She'd sink into swamp, swallowing mud, having it rush inside her eyes, ears, and nose.*

She stepped out of her shoes and stripped off her doctor's coat, its hem and side draining slick mud.

She stumbled again and saved herself from falling by grabbing a willow branch. *Inhale, exhale.* She needed to calm herself. An animal was hurt, dying or dead because of her. But self-sacrifice wouldn't make anything right.

It was getting dark. She should get back in the car. Go to the DeLaCroix's.

With her hands, she shielded her eyes from the sun's final burst of orange. The wood's roots seemed on fire and, for a moment, she was overcome by the forest's primeval nature. *Anything could happen.* She trembled, feeling the mud and fog chilling her bones.

Night creatures were stirring. Bat wings, the scurrying of wild rabbits, the hoot of an owl. She could hear everything. Preternaturally. Even the glide of fish through muddy water, a snake's zig-zag crawl.

From far off, she heard three hollow knockings of gourd. Three calls of a drum.

"Marie." The word ricocheted among trees.

She wanted to run. Shadows were lengthening. She could see the moon's yellow cusp.

She was sinking deeper in damp ground.

Then, she heard her mother. Marie was a child again, on a steamship, churning up the Mississippi.

"Pay attention, Marie."

"Maman?"

"Be alert to your surroundings," her mother scolded. "The smallest details matter."

Marie held her breath. The drums were more rhythmic, softer. Still far away. She crouched, never minding the mud, the wet.

Fireflies were blinking. She looked lower, near tree roots. Noticing the variations in bark and shadow. She could hear her own breath. Air squeezing in and out of her lungs.

She heard another breath, a hushed pant.

"There." Huddled in the shadows.

She stepped as softly and as gingerly as she could. "It's all right. I won't hurt you."

The eyes were small and rounded. Not a big animal. Yet larger than a squirrel or raccoon. Maybe a fox?

"Sssh, let me see you. Let me see."

The creature growled. Marie felt relieved. It was a dog.

"Sssh," she said again, peering, stooping lower. "Let me see you."

A tail thumped the ground.

"You don't have rabies, do you?"

Marie held out her hand, palm open, so the dog wouldn't think she'd strike. "Go on, sniff." The dog did. Marie noticed its tail was like a golden retriever's; its body, black and broad like a Lab's. Ribs were clearly visible. Burrs, dead leaves were twisted in its matted coat.

"You've been lost, on the run, haven't you?"

Its hind leg was bleeding, lying at an odd angle. The dog had dragged it and had probably made the break worse.

"I'm sorry. But I can heal. You understand?"

The dog nuzzled her hand. It was going to be hard carrying the animal back to the car. But she didn't have a choice.

"Good boy. Aren't you a good boy?" She slid her arms under the torso and lifted. The dog's head snapped round to bite her but didn't. "I know. It hurts." She held the animal snug against her chest, trying to step over rock, through uneven, muddy ground as smoothly as she could. She could barely see.

Eh, yé, yé, Maman Marie
Eh, yé, yé, Madame Marie.

The drums drew closer.

"We have to get out of here, dog. Not certain why, just certain we have to go."

She tried to move faster, but it was difficult. If the dog had been less starved, she would've been unable to carry it.

Something was rushing to get them both.

Headlights. She didn't remember turning on her lights. Nonetheless, she was grateful. The light was a beacon.

Her back and her arms ached. Up and up the hill. Dust and pebbles scattered beneath her feet. A few more yards to the road. Her thigh cramped. She almost dropped the dog. Stoic, the animal didn't even whimper. "Good boy. Hold on. We're almost there." Sweating, frightened, dirty, she urged herself on. "... almost there." She heaved one heavy leg, then the other, over the wood tie, onto the roadway.

A shadow ahead of her called, "Babies and dogs. You always rescue the helpless?"

"Reneaux?"

"You look like shit, Doc." It was his car's headlights. "Let me help. I've a way with dogs." True to his word, he gently gathered and cradled the dog.

"What're you doing here?"

"Thought you'd need my help."

"Well, I don't."

"Your car says you do." He aimed the flashlight's beam.

Her car, a new, black Beetle, had been rolled off the road. Upside down, nothing but a tow truck could right it and drag it from the ditch.

"I heard drums, knew people were about—"

"What drums?"

"You didn't hear them?"

"No. Nothing."

"Just like you *see* nothing?"

"That's right. But you're special."

Reneaux wiped dirt from her face. They looked at each other. Marie felt trapped by his eyes. The dog, who'd been resting his head on Reneaux's arm, lifted his head and ears. Marie looked back across the swamp.

"I should take you and this dog home." He opened the car's back door. "Don't want you meeting the DeLaCroixs like a wild woman. Though, knowing them, they might not mind. Witches run in their family." He was behind the wheel.

"Can I have your coat?"

He slipped off his jacket and started the engine. A gun was strapped under his right arm.

Marie, leaning over the front seat, laid the coat on the dog.

Reneaux pressed the gas, the car jerked forward, to the left; its headlights gleamed eerily through the trees, across the bayou swamp.

"There's something else out there."

"Maybe the folks that destroyed your car?" asked Reneaux. "If it's more than two or three, I might not be able to help. Is it? More than two or three?"

She peered into the shadows. The moon hovered on the horizon. The dog howled. *Marie felt a constriction in her heart.*

"It's more than three. We should leave."

Reneaux put his car in reverse, then completed the turn. The car was pointing west, back toward the highway. Marie patted the dog. She looked out the rear window. Lights were swaying. Torches? *She sensed evil.* The car bounced fitfully over the dirt road.

"You shouldn't have come out here alone, Marie."

"I know." She peered into the darkness. East, down that road, were the baby's people.

Marie faced forward when Reneaux turned onto Highway 51.

And, strangely enough, that made them her people, too.

A stranger's soul can be made whole.

For a voodooienne *to heal herself, it requires the most extra-ordinary care.*

—*The Voodoo Companion,* 1865

"Y ou should've been a vet."

"Thought about it." They were in her apartment; the dog, sedated on her bed. She'd have to throw away the covering; she'd never be able to rid it of the swamp smell, the mud and dried blood. She'd set the bone, cleaned the gnash on the dog's foreleg, and wrapped it in gauze.

"Want to bathe him?"

"Later. In the kitchen, there's a small tub and rags. We can wipe him down for now, get the bulk of the dirt off."

"Why didn't you?" Reneaux asked.

"What?"

"Become a vet?"

"Don't know, really." Marie stroked the dog. Eyelids fluttering, his paws clawed the air. *Was he dreaming? Remembering being scared, chased onto the road? And he* had *been chased, just as she'd been.* "You going to get that soap?"

"Yeah. Will do, *Chérie.*"

"Don't call me that." "Chérie." *She could see Jacques grinning, impish, his shirt flying in the humid air.*

"Not even a southern 'honey chile'?"

"No."

"Northern women sure are tough. Or is it just northern doctors?"

"Neither. Just me."

"Right." Reneaux looked at her, sitting rigid, on the bed, her hand sliding over the dog's ribs.

"Formality. I've got it. *Doctor* Levant. Maybe the rare, colloquial, 'Hey, Doc.' I'll remember that. Keep the pecking order straight. Never no mind what we've been through together."

"We've haven't been through anything."

"Sure. Didn't almost get killed together. Didn't rescue you and a dog. Didn't have a dog leak blood on my jacket, in my car."

"The car isn't yours. Police property."

"Who says?"

Marie shook her head. Reneaux wasn't a big man but he seemed big. Filling up the space in her head, getting beneath her skin, making her feel in the wrong. "I should've been a vet."

"Yeah. Spend all day talking with the animals, no? They'd understand you good."

"Water. Soap. Please, Reneaux."

He walked toward the kitchen. "Only going 'cause you said 'please,'" he shouted over his back. Then he kept walking, muttering, "Southerners respect good manners. Please. Thank you. But no 'honey chile.' No '*chérie*' for northern women. No getting too close."

Marie smiled. Reneaux exasperated her yet made her laugh.

She tugged burrs from the dog's fur. She'd have to get his coat shaved. Given the city's heat and humidity, she thought the dog probably wouldn't mind. Bald-headed. Bald-legged. Puff balls of fur behind its ears.

Marie didn't know why she'd become a doctor. A healer, she'd always been that. Birds, mice, crickets, even snakes, she brought home to their two-story walk-up. Her mother never seemed to mind.

Her foster parents did. They beat it out of her. "Creatures remain outdoors." And what couldn't hop, skip, or run, they drowned. Floating creatures in a plastic bucket. She'd be left to bury them in dirt.

But that didn't explain her switch to people. Didn't explain why she filled out one application and left the other one blank. She could be in Virginia, doing her residency on horses, small animals, creatures with scales, shells, and wings.

People were messy, complicated. They talked back, were unpredictable. Hit a dog, it would either go belly-up or fight. When the struggle was over, it was over. People held grudges, memories.

"Here."

"Thanks."

"He's coming round."

She'd hurt a dog. An accident, not malice. Still—amazingly, the dog had trusted her enough to allow her to carry him out of the swamp.

A cool nose nudged her hand. "Hey there," murmured Marie.

The dog had velvet eyes. They were veiled with pain, drugs; nonetheless, the smooth brown contrasted with the steel-black fur. Eyes shut, with some weight on him the dog would look menacing. His eyes open, you'd have to believe some gentle soul had come back from the dead, reincarnated into the light. He licked her palm.

Marie wiped her eyes. She didn't know what was the matter with her; part of her just wanted to sit and cry. Bury her face in the animal's fur and cry for a mother and memories she'd never known. Ten to eighteen—no mother to explain blood between her legs, no mother to explain love, boys, surviving in school. Feeling ugly, too fat, gangly like a colt. No mother to see the beauty in her.

She squeezed water from her rag. "This won't hurt." The dog closed its eyes and went limp. She wiped along the dog's spine. Fur, dried leaves, burrs, and tarlike mud clung to the rag. Smaller wounds, punctures the diameter of a pen or penknife, scars an inch or two long. Someone had tortured the dog, not enough to kill, but enough to hurt.

"Let me help." With the dog in the middle, she and Reneaux stroked the animal clean. He lay, paws up, belly exposed. Utterly trusting.

"I'm sorry. You helped both of us. Me. Dog."

"Never no mind." Reneaux kept wiping, dipping the rag in water, squeezing out dirt, stroking the dog calm.

"Don't know why you annoy me."

"My mother says the same thing. Says I drive her crazy. But she loves me. 'Her big ole baby boy,' no?" He slapped his thigh. Startled, the dog jerked onto its side, its head up.

Marie giggled at the image of Reneaux, an overgrown infant, tough and bawling. "You love her. A lot."

"Sure 'nough." Then he patted the dog. "Ssssh. Don't mind me."

"Any brothers? Sisters?"

"A brother once. He's dead now." Reneaux stopped moving and Marie marveled again at how he seemed like a stop-motion character. Hand poised midair above the dog, head bowed, his entire body was preternaturally still.

"You didn't ask." He moved rhythmically again, stroking the dog.

"What?"

"For details. Usually everyone wants details."

"Not me. Death is private." *She blinked and saw her mother stretched as if sleeping on the kitchen floor.* She pointed at the dog. "What should we call him?"

"We? He's your dog."

"I'm not certain my lease allows a dog."

"You'll have to move, then."

"Very funny. Dog. Let's just call him 'Dog.'" The animal nuzzled her hand.

"He likes it. Dog." Reneaux scratched his head. "*Dog?* Didn't you tell me not to say that?"

"This is different. This *is* a dog. A good dog. A kind dog. 'Kind Dog.' That's it. I'll call him Kind Dog. Remember the picture books? Tiny. No bigger than the palm of your hand. There were dozens of them—*Ant and Bee. Ant and Bee and the Rainbow. One, Two, Three with Ant and Bee.* They had a friend, Kind Dog. They gave Kind Dog a birthday party. Party hats, balloons, a cake made from bones. My mother used to read them. Read me stories from all over the world. Eloise. Ananzi. Peter Rabbit. But the stories she told from her childhood were best."

Marie could hear her mother's voice, soft and sweet, telling tales of yellow moons, hanging moss, and the clicking of cicadas. Telling tales of a woman powerful enough to hold Death at bay:

"Marie, child, she could touch a child's brow, and lift the fever right up into her hand. Once a man near death, chest aching, lungs choking on fluid, called for the Virgin, but it was 'She who Worships the Old and the New' who told him, 'Hush, go to sleep,' and when he woke, his fever was gone, his lungs clear."

But her mother didn't tell the tales often—only on special occasions, when she was morose, tired of the harsh winters. When she mourned for southern heat and languid nights. Or when there was not enough to eat, and distracting tales were needed to fill them up. Marie doubted the stories were true. More like legends, folktales.

"They called her, call her Queen. Queen—"

"—what?"

Her mother wouldn't tell.

Reneaux was staring at her, as if she were crazy, out of her mind.

She said harshly, "Policemen don't say 'dog.'"

"Right," he drawled. "Not tough enough."

The dog whimpered.

"You smoke?"

"No."

"Gauloises?" He lifted the blue pack off the nightstand.

"A friend's," she said, bothered she'd hadn't thrown the package away.

"Maybe this belongs to the dead man? I mean, the dead boy.

70

Jacques's?" His hand grazed the pillow and Marie knew he was seeing her and Jacques in bed together.

She flushed.

"Must be interesting, robbing the cradle."

"Why should you care?"

"I don't."

But she could tell the thought of her and Jacques bothered Reneaux. Just as it bothered her that she'd asked him if he cared.

"It's none of your business," she said flatly.

"'Cept for the murder part." He was drawling again: Deep South. His fingers plucked at the plastic.

"I should've thrown them away. I don't smoke. I don't know why I kept them."

"Good thing you did. Look here." He'd gently torn the plastic wrapper and, beneath it, the blue cover. Between the cover and the foil was a match cover. "*'Une goutte de sang noir. Le sang se manifestera.'* Means 'One drop of black blood. Blood will out.' And a cross. Like the markings on the bodies, but more distinct."

She saw Jacques dead. Saw a man's thumb, marking, like a priest, Jacques's forehead. An upside-down cross. Then, an S, hanging over the horizontal line.

Reneaux flipped the cover over. Red letters on a black background: Breezy's.

"That's where the bust-up was?"

"Yes." *Where the baby's mother died,* Marie thought. *Where Jacques died.*

"Right. Got a plastic bag? Might be fingerprints."

"There's an envelope in the drawer."

He slid the match cover into a blue envelope and licked it shut.

"You'll tell me why you went to the DeLaCroix's?"

"Detective time again?"

"Doc, I mean, Doctor Levant—I need to know."

"You already know. You, DuLac, and El lied to me. You knew the baby's family and said nothing."

"Any other reason?"

Marie arched forward. The dog barked. "Am I a suspect?"

"No. But the DeLaCroixs own Breezy's."

"I didn't know."

"You slept with the dead boy—"

"—fucked. Why not say it? I fucked the dead boy."

Reneaux checked off points with his pen. "—became attached to the baby."

Marie was furious. "Is loving a crime? You, El, and DuLac did worse. Never telling me about the baby's family. Never telling Social Services. Antoinette." She clutched his pen and pad. "Never telling me that her family had to have known that their—what?—daughter, granddaughter, sister, niece—died in the family bar. You didn't even tell me. Didn't even give me a chance to prove abandonment. I could've done it. Saved that child."

"I'm doing my job."

"Out," she ordered. *Jacques flashed before her. He was grinning, clutching his shoes.* "Out." Dog hopped off the bed, hobbled down, three-legged.

"My baby's gone."

"It's not your child."

"Don't tell me anything, Reneaux. You, DuLac, El put that baby in foster care."

"She'll be fine."

"How do you know? Can you guarantee it? Get out." She threw his jacket at him. She wanted to scream, rip at his hair. It'd been too much, all of it, her dreams, losing the baby, hurting a dog, being scared.

Reneaux walked toward the bedroom door; the dog, head high, sniffed at him as he passed by.

"I didn't lie," Reneaux whispered.

"Could've fooled me."

Reneaux looked at her straight on. "Lots of coincidences, Doctor Levant. Too many. By rights, you should be a suspect. Investigated. But DuLac—no, you convinced me that you're special. You've got the gift."

"I don't believe in magic."

"Not even haints? Hauntings?"

He *knew,* knew about her dreams. Knees buckling, she rested her hand on the dog's head. Thick, blunt, warm, it helped steady her.

"Marie, don't go after the DeLaCroixs without a police escort."

"Like you? How could I ever trust you?"

He winced, made a half turn and started walking.

She kept still until she heard the apartment door click shut. "Good dog," she said patting the animal's head. "Kind Dog." He was faithful and true.

"Stay," she said to the dog and, remarkably, he did.

She went onto the balcony, but didn't turn on the fake gas lamps.

The street was crowded, bodies weaving, snaking through the streets. Only in New Orleans did day seem like night and night, day.

Reneaux's '88 Cadillac looked woeful. It was black with dents in its side, its back bumper missing. The convertible hood was patched with gray tarp.

Reneaux walked down the landing steps. His jacket was on, zipped, collar up—never mind the blood, the dirt and heat. He looked more like a thief than a cop. A street hood, they'd say in Chicago. Here, in Louisiana, they'd say, "Trouble man," as in, "That man be trouble, mean trouble, make trouble." A man not to be messed with.

Marie stepped back into the shadows. Watching Reneaux, she felt a welling sadness. She liked when he spoke her name. He said it like nobody else, no French accent, just a quick emphasis on the first syllable. The rest of her name caught up by the wind.

"Reneaux," she whispered. She wanted him to turn around like Jacques had and call, *"Chérie."*

Reneaux turned, peered straight into the darkness, as if he knew exactly where she stood on the balcony.

She held her breath.

"Lock the door, Marie. Lock your front door."

Her breath rushed in short bursts. She stumbled backward into her apartment. Kind Dog watched her, then hobbled after her as she raced to the front room, turned the lock and drew the bolt and chain. Three locks. The prior tenants must have felt they needed them. Did she?

She looked down at the dog. "You should be resting." She lifted the gangly mutt like it was a baby. "You smell. My room smells. My bed smells."

The dog panted, laid its head down on the pillow like it was a person.

Marie threw a spare sheet on the other half of the bed. She didn't turn out the lights. Didn't change her clothes. She just lay there, hearing an upbeat strain of jazz and voices (some cursing, shouting; others chattering excitedly). An engine was gunning, and a car squealed away from the curb. "Bastard. *Cochon*," a woman screamed. Then, laughter.

Marie lay knowing the darkness outside was coming in, lifting the curtains with a breeze, casting shapes on the wooden floor. She was scared. Just beyond the window, she felt *someone, something* was out there, stalking her. It was the same feeling she had in the swamp.

"Dog," she thought. "Dog." He was watching her, his eyes bright, fully alert.

"Hey." She tickled his ear. "We'll look out for each other." She inched closer to Dog, wrapping her arm over him like he was a newborn baby. She felt his steady heartbeat, listened to his breath. She kept the nightstand lamp on.

They both went to sleep; the moon soared higher. New Orleans came alive, just outside, beneath her balcony. Lovers, gamblers, thieves, musicians mingled and lied.

For the first time in a long time, Marie didn't dream.

She woke up starved. Limbs heavy, mouth dry, crust in her eyes, she felt as though she were waking from the dead. Kind Dog was still stretched on the bed, watching her. "Hey, don't be giving me the creeps."

Dog licked her cheek. Why did anyone believe animals were dumb?

"You need to pee?"

Kind Dog sat up and Marie, clothes wrinkled, hair plastered flat, helped the dog off the bed. "Come on." They took the elevator instead of the stairs. Outside, on the steps, Marie smelled honeysuckle, and she felt such longing, she doubled over, cramped, heart contracting, trying to catch her breath. Dog whimpered beside her. She exhaled. "Let's go."

She walked, Dog hobbled across the street. It was a misty dawn, quiet like the morning when Jacques had left.

Kind Dog did his business. A drunk walked by. "Clean it up. There's a fine," he slurred.

"Right. Thanks." Kind Dog barked. Marie found some tissue in her back pocket. Almost like caring for a child. Someone else depending on her for food; going outdoors, being cleaned up; vaccinated, being safe and warm.

She watched Kind Dog roll on the thin strip of lawn, snorting, sniffing. Even a broken leg couldn't quash his playfulness. Marie smiled. When had she decided to keep him? Probably when she named him. She swayed. Her hand gripped the tree. There was the whiff of honeysuckle again. It rose all about her—as the heat rose, in humid waves, from the concrete. Baby Doe. The longing didn't go away.

Then she knew, without knowing how she knew, that her mother had lived here. Her mother had said, "South. Down South. I come from down South." But it was here. Marie was sure of it. Louisiana. New Orleans. Honeysuckle was triggering memories. Leading her back to the baby. Straggling revelers ogled her and the dog like they were caged in the zoo.

She'd been distracted by the swamp, Kind Dog. Been distracted by her dreams and fears. She looked around. Early morn, folks were already carrying beer in plastic cups. An acne-scarred girl strummed a banjo. A woman wrapped in gauze and plastic beads waved a sign, TAROT. A man, like the Tin Man's evil twin, stood still as a statue in a silver jumpsuit, silver boots with silver-painted face, arms, and hands. Living in the Quarter wasn't normal. Mixture of saint and sinner. Descendants from both slaves and masters. Spanish conquerors. French rulers. Canadian refugees. American barbarians. African and Caribbean. Blacks and coloreds. The stew blended exotic, corrupt, decadent. Even honeysuckle wasn't native; the Japanese had carted it in on ships.

"We're 'mixed bloods,'" caroled her mother each year, on her and *Marie's birthday.* Marie never understood what her mother meant. But she sensed her mother's secret glee. The knowledge was supposed to be some talisman. *"Mixed bloods. A history of power."* But what power did her mother have? She was just a woman, aging early, trying to survive in a world unkind to women.

Dead almost twenty years and Marie still felt her mother's warm breath, her mother love. She could see her lying, dead, on the floor. She'd just dropped, straight down dead like a black Sleeping Beauty. Except there wasn't any Prince, no one to reach her where she'd gone.

She'd been washing dishes, the water was still running, her hands and arms still damp. Marie didn't know how long she'd lain. Just as she didn't know anything about her people. She only knew her mother loved honeysuckle, knew she lived in Chicago where her mother cleaned houses, trying to provide, and when she died, there was no money, no relatives, little food, and only a few boxes of belongings.

Marie stared at the brightening sky. A swarm of mosquitoes was heading south. Strange. Didn't mosquitoes only rise at night? Swooping in from the swamps, infected with West Nile?

Summer—"killing season," local doctors intoned. West Nile replacing yellow fever. Both carried by the lowly mosquito. Two centuries and nothing had changed. Summer, the dangerous season. Time of disease. Illness. No ease. Time when Nature's small creatures sucked and infected blood.

Marie looked down the narrow street. Homes mixed with businesses. Families and single folks like her, living—trying to live above and between bars, grills, restaurants, blues haunts, porn shops, and less-than-respectable boarding houses. A steamship bellowed. The sun inched higher. Why live here? Downtrodden. Edgy. Fat tourists mixed with lean scammers. Pigeons clamoring over crumbs. A cacophony of music: rock, blues, Latin jazz, pop, big band, Cajun, and zydeco spilled out of bars, loudspeakers above trinket shops. Why here? Mosquitoes, perversely, swarming at dawn. Soft, porous soil supporting centuries of crimes: piracy, slavery, invasion. Church bells competing with sinful revelers. She'd been drawn for a reason.

Her mother had walked these streets. Maybe even given birth here, surrounded by sin. She'd always known New Orleans hadn't been random. *Skin tingling, she remembered being a toddler, drifting to sleep, drifting, drifting to a Creole lullaby. When she was three, her mother pronounced, "English. English. Speak only English." But, in private, she'd never given up the staccato lilt of "Marie." Never stopped praising "mixed bloods."*

Marie needed to find the baby.

Kind Dog whimpered. Hopped a bit to the left.

She made up her mind to call in sick. *Doctor, heal thyself.*

She'd go to Breezy's.

She scratched Kind Dog's ear. "Come on." They started across the deserted street. Dog barked at a squirrel darting, zigzagging across the street.

"You like hunting?" The dog seemed to nod. "Maybe you've got hound in you?"

She felt almost happy. She and Kind Dog rode the makeshift elevator, an iron cage with rudimentary pulleys added in the modern age.

She scrambled eggs, gave half to the dog. He lapped water

while she heated coffee with chicory and milk. She wrapped plastic wrap around the dog's wound.

They both took a shower in an old-fashioned tub where easy women had lounged, bubbles covering their breasts. A circular rail and a plastic curtain converted it into a shower. Kind Dog sat; she stood, a canopy over him, gently washing his back.

She dried herself and the dog off.

She dressed. Jeans. T-shirt. Picked up the phone. "Sick. I'm sick, El."

Marie could almost see El at the nurses' station, tapping her purple nails: "Sure," she finally said, "Sure."

Marie wanted to reassure her that she was all right. But she was still too angry, too hurt. El didn't have to lie about the baby's family. Didn't have to send an innocent to Child Welfare. Marie clicked the receiver without saying, "bye."

She powered up her computer, punched in Breezy's on Map Quest and grabbed her keys. "Let's go." Kind Dog barked.

She stopped. "Shit." Her Volkswagen was belly-up.

A horn blared. She went to the balcony. Reneaux was leaning against his car, passenger door wide open. "I figured you'd want to be moving." He grinned.

Marie wished she had a flowerpot to throw at him. My, he was too handsome. Light shining from behind his back; the crucifix in his ear sparkling. Black car, black jacket, black man. Egypt-beautiful with a good ole boy drawl. No need to leave New Orleans for interesting men. All shades, all accents; multilingual. If that was what she was looking for—but all she ever needed was sex, not love. The baby needed her. Profoundly. Loving her, finding, taking care of her was more important than any man.

"I want to go to Breezy's."

"I figured. Come on down." She and Kind Dog did.

"Here." He handed her beignets, still hot and melting sugar. "Café au lait."

The dog climbed into the backseat.

"Why'd you bring him?"

"Good company." Biting into her beignet, she stared straight ahead. White powder dusted her hands and shirt.

Reneaux shifted the car in gear.

They headed toward the most depressed part of the parish. Beyond the elegant Garden District with its stately manor homes, near the waste dumps—a cesspool, literally, for the city. Gangs. Drugs. Entrenched poverty. More dangerous than usual. But what part of New Orleans was really safe? Homes with manicured lawns had their share of secrets, too. Wife beaters. Child abusers. A variety of sins.

Reneaux slipped in a CD. Nina Simone. "You Put a Spell On Me." As the car sped on, the houses became smaller, more ill-kept. Rats darted across the road. Mosquitoes died on the windshield.

Breezy's was less than sixteen miles from the hospital. Still in St. Charles Parish but a ragtail collection of streets where the poorest of the poor seemed to live.

Marie was even angrier at El's and DuLac's lying. She could've been here in thirty minutes, finding the baby's people. Instead, she'd hurt a dog. Her car was on its back in a ditch. And she'd been scared. Run off.

Here, doors, windows, and drapes were pulled shut, closed southern style against the heat. Indoors, men, women, and children were desperately starving. Or plagued by diabetes, blood pressure, lucky enough to get help from a free clinic. Skipping medicines, cutting pills in two. Children played outdoors in frayed underwear. A sluggish creek edged the community; it was rancid with chemicals from the plastics plant across the river. Who knew what cancers leeched into soil, water? She already knew some of the children were stunted from too much lead. She'd treated dozens for eating paint flaked from windowsills. If this was what her mother had been escaping, she was glad of it.

She was glad, too, that Reneaux had come with her. She probably would've been distracted by sorrow. She would've missed the turn. Missed the black arrow, low to the ground, almost covered by weeds, sunflowers, and black-eyed susans.

They bounced down a dirt road. A hand-lettered sign: BREEZY'S.

The car slowed to a stop on gravel. The low-slung shack, made of whitewashed pine, looked as if a strong wind could knock it down.

She turned toward Reneaux. "I'm not going to say 'I'm sorry.'"

"You were right, Doc. I was wrong."

"El and DuLac, too."

"I'm not going to speak for them. They'd their own reasons. For myself, I'm sorry. I should've told you as soon as I knew about the baby's family."

"Why do you do that?"

"What?"

"Make me angry. Then, make me—"

"What?"

She shook her head. "Like you," she almost said, but she already liked him too much.

"I'm going to make them give me the baby." Marie got out of the car and took one step toward the shack. "Kind Dog. Stay."

She heard Reneaux getting out of the car, stepping like a shadow behind her. She felt relieved.

It wasn't even nine; sweat drained down her back. The building seemed haggard, like an old woman gone to lie down, to soothe her sore back. Nothing but weathered, pockmarked wood. Lopsided windows. A metal-hat exhaust poking into the sky. But she'd be lying if she said she didn't feel evil. Inside, the baby's mother had died. How? Inside, a slew of folks had fought, been knifed, shot, and driven to Charity.

Except for a road sign, there was no marquee, no neon glittering on the shack's roof. It was just a shack, harmless looking, but it radiated sin.

"Former slave quarters," said Reneaux. "Men might've lain here, tired out from hauling cotton to the harbor."

"No, no. This was the women's house." *She didn't know how she knew that.* Somehow she smelled and felt the sweat, spirit of women. Like the few times her mother had taken her to a church—after the service, after kneeling, sitting on hard wood pews, her mother took her downstairs to the kitchen. There, young women, old women, worked in unison kneading dough, flouring chicken, crimping pie. You could feel the specialness of the women, tired out, but soothing each other with soft melodies floating out of their mouths like doves. *Like a trick of the light, the shack shimmered.* She shook herself. She was being silly,

believing DuLac's press. This was a shack. Now a bar. Layered
with crime, greed, and violent pleasures.

She and Reneaux moved toward the blackened windows; she
felt she was being watched. *Ghosts behind those windows.*

She knocked on the door. No sound of scurrying. No creatures about.

Reneaux pounded. "Police. Open up."

Like open sesame, the door swung back on its hinge. There
didn't seem to be anyone. Just a pit of vile-smelling darkness.

"It's the hooch. Shine. Whiskey."

"Something more." She coughed. Urine, feces, but still something else. Marie told herself it was her doctor's senses making
her so sensitive. There was some chemical, man-made, not
organic smell. Or was it the reverse? *Some unfamiliar, organic
smell. Primeval. Latent in the darkness.*

Marie stepped inside.

"Wait." Reneaux reached for her just as men rushed them from
both sides and grabbed her, pulling her farther into the room.

Marie felt their hands on each arm, twisting, forcing her down to
the floor. Thick, punishing hands. She tried to resist and cried out.

"Police. Let her go," Reneaux called. "Let her go or I'll shoot."

Someone kicked the door closed, blotting out the light. A
hand clamped over Marie's mouth and one of the men leaned
his full weight on her, pushing her to the floor. His weight was
suffocating, his hands like her foster parent's hands, trying to
snatch her spirit. She couldn't breathe. She was a child again,
helpless; they were powerful.

Marie raged, digging her nails into the man's arm, biting
down on his hand.

A flashlight pierced the dark. Reneaux grabbed one of the men.

"Let go of me," she screamed, her rage and hatred bubbling up from childhood memories.

"Fools. Do as she says. Let her go this instant." A candlestick moved, disembodied in the darkness. "Put away your gun, Reneaux. You think it gives you power here?"

Caught in the candle's glow, Marie saw an ancient face. Not much more than a skull. Skin tight, glowing translucent in the candlelight. Blue veins like tentacles reaching across the brow and temples.

"Be better off dead, *non?*"

Marie didn't flinch.

"Hah. *Bon femme.* Not frightened of death. Turn on the light, fools. Don't you know who she be? Don't you know?" The woman blew out her candle.

The man beside her clicked off his flashlight.

Yellow lights buzzed overhead. The bar's walls were blood red. Peanut shells littered the ground, dead beetles, roaches, too. The bar was lacquered black. There was a small stage, a drum set, mikes, a guitar, and a metal washboard, almost like armor, except it made music when worn, slapped or scratched with nails. There weren't any tables or chairs. This was a place for drinking and dancing—bodies packed tight enough, the room dark enough, no one could tell (or care) who was stroking and touching whom.

Out of the corner of her eye, Marie saw movement. A haze swelling, taking form. Will-o'wisps, waifs shuffling between rows of cots.

"You all right, Marie?"

She nodded. "You?"

Reneaux shrugged, wiped blood from his nose. His jacket half pulled off, Marie could see his gun, locked in its holster.

"No more violence here." The voice was reedy, but powerful.

Three men, ugly, thick like bulldogs, backed away from her and Reneaux.

The woman wore a red and gold chignon and Marie could almost imagine her skin once fair. Beautiful, creamy-white like the baby's mother. She was petite, small-boned, like the man beside her. But it was clear that the man dressed in a red silk shirt, looking like a retired jockey, was the escort. Caretaker. The woman was in charge. The boss. A contradiction. Elegant in a chantilly lace and rose silk dress. Elegant in a gown her ancestors would've worn. A black ribbon of smoke trailing from her candle. Her satin shoes stepping on filth.

"I could arrest them." Reneaux pointed at the bulldog men.

"But you won't."

"I should."

"What you expect, sneaking up? My men thought you was going to rob me."

"You call, 'Open up, Police' sneaking?"

The woman cackled.

Marie stepped forward. "Madame." Inexplicably, she bobbed a small curtsy. "We've come about your great-granddaughter."

"*Je n'ai pas de petite-fille.*"

Marie looked to Reneaux. He shook his head, mournful.

"I don't understand."

"You understand my Creole well enough. No great-grandchild. *Non.* None."

"I held her in my arms."

"*Oui,* your arms good for holding babies."

"Making them, too," said one of the men.

"Shut up." Reneaux jerked forward; Marie clutched his arm.

Marie's eyesight had adjusted. There were other people. A freckle-faced bartender. Another man, stocky like a defensive linebacker; and another, with dreads and a lazy, out-of-place smile.

"Mind if we look around?" asked Reneaux.

"Got a warrant?"

"You going to be difficult?"

"You come to see if I had a baby, *non?* So why you need to look around?"

"You've known about the baby all along," blurted Marie.

The woman spoke, scornful. "You think I don't know what you want?"

The two stared. Ashamed but not knowing why, Marie lowered her gaze. The woman smiled, tight-lipped yet pleased. The jockey man seemed disappointed. The man with dreads smiled wider.

Marie knew she'd lost ground. But she had no clue about the territory. No sense of the terrain's mysteries.

"What else you looking for? Drugs? Money? Check the cash box. You can dip your hands like the other police. Firearms? Everyone has a permit. I even got a permit for this." She pulled a pearlized derringer from a fold in her gown. "Small but dangerous. Keeps me safe. From bad men. Weak men. Gamblers. Corrupt cops. Good cops trying for redemption. *Non?*"

Reneaux kept his face blank. But Marie saw the clutch of his hands, the slight contraction of his jaw. He'd been insulted, hurt deep.

"Have you told this child your tale?"

Reneaux's back bowed. Marie wanted to defend him, but she

didn't know from what. She attacked: "How can you say the baby isn't your kin?"

"How can you say it is?"

Marie stepped closer and the bulldog men shadowed her. "Don't you have a granddaughter?"

"*Non.* Marie-Claire—"

The girl's name.

"—used to be."

"What do you mean? She is or she isn't."

"I'm tired. Need to lie down." She turned, her gait slow. The jockey man offered his arm.

"Marie-Claire was here the night she died."

"*Non.* She wasn't here."

"There was a big fight. They dropped her at Charity with the other bodies."

"Not here. She wasn't here. Never here."

"You're telling the truth?"

"Why should I lie, girl?" the woman screeched, looking like an ancient fury.

"You lied about the great-grandchild."

"*Non.* I disowned my granddaughter. Nothing she be, nothing she do be a part of me."

Harsh, unforgiving. Marie felt Madame's anger like a weight, a wall collapsing.

"Maybe we'll speak to your daughter."

"You do that." She scuttled forward. "But don't let her claim that baby. Better baby die first than be given to her."

"You're afraid of her. The daughter?" Soon as she said it, Marie knew it was true.

Eyes wide, hands flailing, Madame screamed, "*Cochon.* You're no one. Ignorant girl. Don't even know how to use your power."

"Madame." The jockey man clasped her hand. "You need to lie down. Let me help."

The old woman was trembling, muttering Creole.

Marie understood snatches. Malice mixed with regret, disappointment. "Broken." "Blood too red." "Spirit snatch"; no, "steal." "Steal the spirit." "Undo the line." "Mixed blood."

On the far right, someone moved. There was a door. Another room. A man was hiding in the doorway, shadowed, his hand on the frame. He pulled back inside the room; his ring finger glinted, catching shards of light. No one else saw him. Or else Madame's men were covering for him.

Marie shuddered. *She saw Jacques, on a mattress, on the floor, his knees to his abdomen.*

"Let's go. Madame DeLaCroix's no use." Reneaux's hand was on his gun. The men in the room had edged closer, protective of Madame.

"No." Marie moved close enough to smell the woman's breath. Laudanum. A nineteenth-century opiate. Sweet and bitter.

"You've got to let me have the baby. I'll care for her. It's a girl, did you know? Your bloodline. *Ta lignée.*"

The woman sucked spittle, hissed like a cat. The jockey man stared at the floor, his head shaking from side to side.

"Admit your family has abandoned her. Simple. That's all. I'll adopt the baby and care for her."

A hand reached out; Marie flinched. The woman stared and Marie shifted her weight into the back of her heels, feeling like the woman was draining, sucking the life out of her. The woman

90

looked away this time, but again Marie felt she'd come out the worse. She'd lost some ground.

"Don't you care where the baby is?" Marie screamed.

"*Non.*"

The bar men were edging closer, looking at Marie like she was crazy.

"Come on, Marie."

"No."

The jockey man blocked her. "Madame's tired. Too tired for this." His voice was soft, strangely comforting.

"I need to make sure the baby's fine."

"She's fine. True. *C'est vrai.*"

Marie wanted to believe him.

"*Vite.* Go away," screeched the woman, her hand raised midair. She began to sing:

> Guéde, Guéde, have mercy,
> Don't let me lose my way.
> Guéde, Guéde,
> Don't let me lose my way.

Then, her song switched:
> *Fais dodo, mon piti bébé.*
> *La lune toute jaune, se lève.*
> *Fais dodo, mon piti bébé.*

Marie kept stepping backward, like she was being pushed, a consistent pressure moving her out of the bar.

A mist clouded her eyes, then cleared. Women in rough shifts were lying on cots: some curled, knees to their chest; some spread-eagled, bodies defenseless; some on their bellies, hands tucked beneath them. Some were crying, their mouths open with silent wails. Some, slack-jawed, rocked; some twitched, batted at the air. Women from another age.

"Doc. Marie? You okay?"

She felt drained. *What happened?*

"Breathe."

The men laughed. Her heart raced, skipping beats.

Reneaux's arm was steadying her. "Let's go."

Someone clicked off the lights. Marie felt ill-prepared.

The old woman was gone. Disappeared like a ghost. No sound of shuffling, just absence. A depression in the shadows.

"Did you see him?" she whispered, urgent. "He turned off the lights."

"Who?"

In the back room. Something glinting between the door and frame. Her knees buckled. "I've lost the baby," Marie moaned.

"Come, let me get you out of here."

An ambulance wailed. A wail meant disaster, distress, but it called to Marie's heart. Like a siren luring her upon the rocks. No doubt the ambulance was on its way to Charity. She needed to go where she'd be more useful. She was a doctor. She could heal. Or at least try.

Reneaux led her outside into the light; Marie shielded her eyes.

* * *

Pandemonium both outside and in. Ambulances were lined up at the door. The hospital ER was already crowded. Sunday,

10:00 A.M. Nowhere else to go for a bad hangover, strep throat, cancer spreading through your lungs, or worsening diabetes. The halls overflowing with the poor, sick, and weary. Churches and hospital. Both guaranteed to overflow on Sundays.

K-Paul, freckled face sweating, was shouting, directing traffic. "Morgue. He's dead." "Critical." "Him up to surgery." "Huan, stitches."

"Why didn't you leave him at home?" K-Paul asked, looking at Kind Dog.

"I said the same thing," muttered Reneaux.

"Never occurred to me." Marie shrugged on her resident's coat.

"Knew you were strange." K-Paul lifted a sheet. "Another morgue stop."

"Dogs aren't allowed in a hospital," complained El.

"Seeing-eye dogs are," said Huan, rolling a gurney into treatment.

"Yeah. He's helping me see."

"Humpf," said El, arms crossed against her broad chest.

"Okay, Sully, keep him out front, at your desk. Please. For me?"

"Sure. Come on, boy." Kind Dog looked at Marie; she nodded; he trotted off.

"I'm glad you're here." DuLac's gloves were already speckled with blood.

"Me, too." *Be a doctor and heal.*

She snapped on gloves.

"Room Three," said El. "Chest wound. Stabbing."

Adrenaline kicked in. Marie forgot about Reneaux, Kind Dog, and the baby. Forgot about an old woman hating her daughter and afraid to love her great-grandchild. In seconds, she was probing a wound, rough from serrated edges—a kitchen knife? The boy was unconscious, his face smooth and bland like a sleeping angel's.

"What happened?"

"Brawl at Saint Mary's High. Glad you skipped your unplanned leave."

Marie overlooked the sarcasm. She began packing the wound while El tackled the IV lines.

The curtains parted. DuLac peered at her handiwork. "Call upstairs. He'll live. Saunders, stitch him."

"Young." Marie stared at the face, baby fat still in the cheeks.

"*Oui*, Miz Marie. The young keep feeding on each other. Soon won't be any left."

"We'll save this one." El dashed by, swinging open the ringed curtains.

Marie had a wide view of the hospital. Some kids blaring boom box hip-hop. Bodies on gurneys in the halls, in rooms, treatment stations; some even stacked near the elevator doors. A blur of nurses, doctors in white, medics, technicians in blue focusing on kids wounded and dying. The ER ambulance arrival door was still flung open. Heat wafted into the ER. If he was here, Severs would be shouting, "Air-conditioning costs money, people." But the ambulances were abandoned, parked haphazardly, their doors flung open, forlorn and empty, displaying their life-support systems. Sirens off, the emergency lights still swirled red, yellow like an odd disco ball, making eerie patterns on the hospital linoleum.

"What is it?" DuLac was staring at her.

Someone had been left. She was sure of it. She sprinted across the room. Looked inside the nearest ambulance, then the next, and the next. In the last vehicle, not even on a gurney, but stretched out on the metal floor, was a girl. Sixteen, seventeen? Her pale face was made up, almost grotesque with bright blue shadow, purple lips, and red circles of rouge. Her hair was in tiny cornrows. Her dress was blue with lace, old-fashioned like Marie-Claire's. Like Madame DeLaCroix's.

Marie was furious. How could the medics have left her here? Dead or not, she shouldn't have been forgotten.

"Medic," she screamed.

"Need help?"

"Aw, Reneaux. They just left her. Just left her here—"

"—like a dog?"

"No, worse." Marie tugged at the girl's arm, trying to lift her body.

"Wait." Reneaux squeezed into the ambulance. He squatted. "Look." He lifted her left shoulder. "A tattoo. Similar to the dust markings on the other bodies. An inverted cross with a snake instead of Christ."

"Some ritual?"

"Or made to look that way. Leave the girl here."

"What do you mean?"

"This is a crime scene. Someone dumped the body."

"She wasn't forgotten?"

"No. Look at her. Known any medic not to use a litter? 'Sides, does she look dressed for school?"

"No. Looks like she's been at a costume party. Some kind of ball."

"It ain't Mardi Gras," said Reneaux.

95

"She was a pretty girl," murmured Marie, staring at the blue satin slippers, the cameo necklace accenting her breasts. Her appearance was out of sync, dressed for the wrong century.

"No apparent bruises from a brawl. No knife wounds." Reneaux scribbled on his pad.

"Dumped?" It was DuLac.

"Appears so," said Reneaux. "I'll call it into the station. We should leave her, Doc. This is a possible crime scene now. Might be some prints."

Reluctantly, Marie backed out of the ambulance. "Doesn't seem right to leave her."

"Only way to catch her killer."

"Miz Marie, your sight wrought magic again."

"Intuition, DuLac."

"Yet infallible."

"If that were true, I'd have known you were lying to me for the last two months."

"I'm not your enemy, Marie. I had reasons for not telling you about the DeLaCroixs. Good reasons."

"I don't believe you."

"Let's have dinner tonight. Me, you, El, Reneaux. I cook a fine gumbo."

"No. Not ever."

"Doctor Levant." Reneaux was drawling again, the good ole southern boy charm. "Three women dead. Your friend Jacques." He said "friend" without any sarcasm. "There's a pattern here. At dinner, we can talk about it. Maybe solve this puzzle."

"Only puzzle I care about is getting Baby Doe—home. My home."

"I understand."

"No, you don't, DuLac."

Reneaux bent toward her ear. "Settle down, Doc. Marie. Give him a chance."

DuLac looked sad-eyed, and Marie felt furious at herself for feeling sorry for him.

"I can't."

"You mean you won't? When the baby's yours, and it will be one day—my only prophecy—you going to tell her you didn't help find her mother's killer?"

Marie trembled. DuLac's words hurt. Part of her didn't care about the murdered mother. She wanted the baby. Safe. With her. But how could she, a doctor, not care about death from un-natural causes? She did care. All the murdered girls could've been her baby, her baby grown into a young woman, then killed for no reason. Some other doctor would be pondering why another young girl had to die.

DuLac towered over her. He whispered, "Don't you know New Orleans be the City of Sin?"

Wonderingly, Marie stared at him.

Reneaux murmured, "I'm positive more people are going to die."

"Women," Marie answered, knowing it was true. "More women are going to die." Jacques was an anomaly—she was sure of it.

Marie looked back at the body. There wouldn't be any sirens for a forensic team. Just more men inspecting this poor girl. *Inspecting?* Why'd she think that?

In her mind's eye, she could see the girl undressed on a bed . . .

*undressed on a steel examining table. In each case, she was sur-
rounded by men.*

Reneaux was watching her, sympathetic, concerned. DuLac's
face was a mask.

"Eight o'clock?"

The glass doors slid open. She stopped midway through.

"Reneaux, is a pregnancy test standard procedure?

DuLac exhaled: "You think?"

"I don't know what I think. The other women—" she
stopped, words catching in her throat.

"Murdered," said Reneaux. "The ones murdered?"

Marie nodded. "Were they checked for pregnancy?"

"Why would you think that?" DuLac asked.

"I don't know."

"If not," said Reneaux, "we'll get a court order to exhume
them. Easy enough."

In New Orleans, bodies were buried above ground. Marie had
never visited a Louisiana cemetery, but she imagined crypts de-
scribed by Poe. Walled-off tombs; possibly babies, fetuses, dying
in their mother's abdomen. Buried twice over. Damn, she was
becoming morbid.

"See you after the shift." The automatic doors slid shut. The
air conditioner buzzed. She'd scream if she spent another second
standing over a dead body with Reneaux and DuLac.

* * *

Tired, hungry, Marie entered notes on a little girl's chart. Ear
infection left too long. Pus-filled canals. She'd write a pre-
scription, a recheck, then be gone, downstairs to the cafeteria
for a four-o'clock lunch. Only egg salad would be left. Maybe

a tuna salad. Neither her favorite. At least the coffee would be hot.

"Doctor Levant."

They were exiting the elevator: Severs and a tall man, six-four, maybe even six-five, dressed splendidly in a double-breasted suit, a silk kerchief in his pocket.

Heat washed through her. Pheromones. Cheeks flush. Her heart rate up. Body chemistry encouraging her to mate. Nothing but lust.

Marie nudged El. Almost five hours they'd worked, side by side. Professional. Polite. More than she cared to admit, Marie missed their easy camaraderie.

"What do you think, El?"

El frowned. "Not my type."

"He's the best-looking man I've seen all day."

"You're a fool then. Reneaux's got more charm in his earring than this overdressed fool."

"I think you've got a crush."

"Humpf."

"Doctor Levant," called Severs.

Bemused by El's perverseness, Marie walked, taking her time, weaving between patients, wheelchairs, gurneys, and abandoned IV trees. She was being watched. Taking her time, gave her more time to watch him.

He was midnight black. Blacker than black. Much as she admired Severs, she knew he had his own form of racial prejudice, his bias against dark-skinned folks. She'd read history. Tales explaining how New Orleanians still considered descendants of nineteenth-century free coloreds (often the bastard children of

French aristocrats) as superior. A white relation and white skin seemed to insure status and wealth, property, and deference. Two hundred and fifty years later, folks like Severs were still jealously guarding their privileges, fawning over those whose light skin marked them as fellow members. The man beside Severs had some other power beyond color.

Handsome, darker than Reneaux—almost as if in the very darkness of him, you could see shadows and images of African glory.

Marie had always had a healthy appetite for sex. She'd lain with men, a whole host of colors. A sexual rainbow. Color didn't matter, it was always some energy, some quality that attracted her. Jacques had been sensual on the dance floor, good-spirited, good-hearted. But she'd always been attracted to the strong, those who worked out, buffing their bodies, or even those, dressed as office men, who nonetheless exuded control, vision, adept at political, corporate power. She felt a contraction in her abdomen. This man, standing so nonchalantly beside Severs, was silently calling her name.

Severs was speaking, his words floating away. Marie paid him no more mind than a shoo-fly. His companion was luring her. Some outrageous energy poured out of him, promising sweet nights. She stopped short. No, not sweet.

Up close, she could see the skeleton beneath his face.

He clasped her hand.

She felt the violence. Like the time there'd been a storm and a wire cracked, whipping downward, twisting, snaking, snapping at her legs, her lace-tipped socks and black shoes. She'd screamed. The air was filled with a deadly charge. It was sheer luck she hadn't been touched.

But now she felt as though she had. Touched by a malevolent force. Electrified beyond redemption.

She kept her expression bland.

"Doctor," he murmured.

She tilted her head, listening for the sound beneath the sound, the meaning behind the word "doctor." Subtext, nuance. Nothing was as it seemed.

No, not sweet. This man could never, ever be sweet.

He squeezed her hand—quick, hard. She bristled. He smiled and she had an overwhelming sense that he'd issued a challenge.

Severs was grinning like Christmas. Much as she appreciated Severs, she deplored his tactics. This meeting had less to do with her as a doctor, more to do with her being a woman. Why not Huan? Or Meredith?

"I have work."

"Monsieur Allez, trustee president, stopped by to visit us."

"You mean check up on us?" Now she understood Severs's obsequiousness. Keep Monsieur Allez happy. How many other women—doctors, nurses—had been trotted out for Allez's inspection?

"As you see, Monsieur Allez, we need everything. Technicians, beds, supplies. IV lines. Linens. Can't your board provide more money? People are suffering, dying. Steal if you have to—" (She didn't know why she said "steal.")

"Steal? Surely not." Not a southern drawl, nor Creole or Cajun patois. Crisp, clear, standard English—the kind from good prep schools and New England colleges. In medical school, she'd met plenty of self-satisfied sons of privilege. Just not too many black ones.

"As in Robin Hood. Getting the rich to provide for the poor."

"We hold charity balls. Auctions. Wrangle from city government."

"You can ask the mayor."

"A friend of mine."

"It ought to be simple, then. More effective than expensive entertainments for the rich, which may or may not raise much money for charity."

His gaze seemed to pinion her like a butterfly. She was under a microscope; her assets being catalogued and measured.

Then, Allez's body relaxed. Too much so. The opposite of Reneaux, who went still, his muscles tense. Foolishly, she couldn't help smiling. She excited him.

Severs spoke. "Doctor Levant, perhaps you'd like to show Monsieur Allez around."

"No. I've got work." Never mind lunch.

Severs coughed.

Marie felt almost sorry for him. He was a sycophant. Dangerous, if he thought he could manipulate her. Severs's only saving grace was his love for the hospital.

"Please, Doctor Levant. I'd enjoy spending time with you."

Allez's face was angular. Sweeping high cheekbones. A broad brow, shapely eyes, nose. Lips like soft black clouds.

"More people need my care than you."

He shrugged, stretched out his hand, palm upraised. A false vulnerability.

She'd lost her appetite. "I need to get back to work."

"I hope we meet again."

"Collector," she thought. She could tell by the sound of his voice. She kept walking, not looking back. He might or might not have found her really attractive, but, now, since she'd rebuffed him, he'd feel compelled to collect her.

She overheard Severs apologizing for her behavior, intoning about the stress of ER, dedicated doctors, and sleep deprivation. She didn't hear Allez's response.

"What've you got for me, El?"

"An unwed mother with no prior prenatal care. A drunk who had a bottle smashed into his head. A boy with burns on his hands. Said he'd been playing with matches. Looks like cigarette burns to me."

"Hell." Marie took the charts. "Call Social Services." She hoped Marie-Claire's baby—no, her baby—wasn't being hurt.

She turned. Allez was by the elevator, still watching her.

An unbidden thought: *Jacques would never have hurt her— this man—would.*

She thought about calling Reneaux. What would she say? This man frightened her? No more than a handshake and she felt inexplicable terror.

Since being in New Orleans, her dreams made her feel weak, disoriented. Thoughts she couldn't control multiplied in her mind like worms.

She looked back over her shoulder.

It was Allez who'd orchestrated the meeting. Allez—who'd used Severs as the pawn.

Allez clasped Severs's hand, and the diamond on his right finger glinted down, then up. Light fractured on the ceiling.

She turned with a vengeance. "You were at Breezy's. This morning. Hiding in the back room."

His expression hardened. "I don't hide."

"Why wouldn't he be at Breezy's? He owns it," said Severs.

Allez slowly smiled, but the effect was grotesque. A smile ill-suited to his eyes that dared—*what?* Dared her to be his adversary? Dared her to call him a liar?

She was scared. But Allez reminded her of all the men and boys who'd tried to take advantage of a vulnerable foster care girl.

"I don't believe you." She felt his fury, tangible like smoke in the air.

"Welcome to my world," he murmured, and she walked away, slowly, sedately. Inhale, exhale. Swallowing bile, quelling her nausea, Marie wondered how it'd come to this—all she wanted to do was to love a child.

Marie ached from lifting, bending over bodies, from scurrying from one crisis to the next. The burned boy confessed: "Ramie did it." A teenager bullying an eight-year-old. Marie was relieved. No parental abuse. No foster care. Instead, a sweet boy with two parents swearing he wouldn't be harmed again.

Marie was happy for him. He was loved. Too bad no one had loved the murdered girls. At least loved them enough to protect them. They'd only been loved enough (or abused enough) to become pregnant.

Reneaux called. They'd all been pregnant. One, six weeks. Another eight. One, thirteen, entering the second trimester. Coroners had filed it in their reports. Of the three, only Marie-Claire had had a viable babe.

But other than the usual flood of get-well calls, no one called the hospital looking for an underage girl. A missing daughter?

An absent niece? A cousin lost with no ID? Just unidentified cases of good girls (or, maybe, bad girls?) gone dead.

Reneaux said there'd been no missing person reports filed. Bad or good, saint or sinner—how could so many women die and nobody care?

Easy. She remembered her own history. None of the neighbors cared about her and her mother. No relatives claimed her. No one wore black and sang about the righteous Lord. Or flying off to glory.

Social Services had buried her mother in a pauper's grave. No memorial. No newspaper photo and obituary. Her foster mother just announced, "It's done," like her mother was so much dirt. Thrown away, cast off. "Done." Encased in wood. Baked in soil. No one in the world would ever know she existed. No one would ever know a soul was lost during Chicago's driest heat, or know about a little girl's memory of arriving home too late and holding her mother's still-wet hand.

When she was eighteen, her caseworker gave her a copy of her file, a box with her mother's effects and the location of her grave. The "L" trip was far—way beyond the city's edge. Past picket fence suburbs, rural shacks, plants spewing smoke and the city dump.

Trudging over snow-packed ground, she'd searched for her mother. She, too, was Marie. With her bare hands, she wiped headstones, pulled back dry weeds, scratched crusted dirt. Marie Winters. Marie Pulaswoski. Marie Ann. Old women—one, dead in the 1920s; another, dead in 1983; and an infant, dead in 1885.

Nearing sundown, she found the small brick square pressed into the ground, covered with snow, pebbles, and twigs. MARIE

LEVANT NÉE CROSS, 1948–1980. On her knees, her nose blue, her hands and feet tingling with pain, she tried to feel her mother's spirit.

She opened the mahogany box. Inside was a pin, snakes entwined about a tree, and a drawing of a snake eating its own tail. Her birth certificate listed Father: Unknown. Mother: Marie. Her place of birth: scratched out. Hospital: covered in black ink. A piece of paper saying nothing.

Did her mother or someone else alter the birth certificate? Was it done before or after her mother died?

There was another sheet: her mother's death certificate. Marie never looked at it but she couldn't bring herself to throw it away. She lay the paper face down atop her birth certificate.

She dug inside the velvet pouch and pulled out a rosary. Black pearl. On the crucifix, Christ had a snake—the Devil, the same Devil who'd tempted Eve, taunted Him in Gethsemane, entwined about His feet. There were two pictures—one of a pink Virgin, blonde and blue-eyed. The other brown—not a traditional Virgin, but still compelling, posed like a goddess, a would-be saint. Sitting slightly in profile, her hair pulled into a chignon, her eyes slanted, casting a sideways glance, Marie felt she drew upon some supernatural power. *Voudon Marie* was written on the back of this picture; *Mary*, on the other.

Her mama had raised her to be a good Catholic. Yet the crucifix and the brown Virgin were blasphemous. Evil.

There was a folded note; inside it, her mother's flowing script:

All things alive.

She dropped the rosary in the pouch, slid in the wrinkled pictures, and as she replaced the note, she saw more writing, less neat, elegant, as if the writer's hand had been trembling:

Snakes are stirring in my blood. Yours, too.

She'd closed the box, feeling she'd some sin to repent. She swore she'd never open it until she did some good in the world. Became a doctor. Fully certified. She'd make her mother proud. Dispel the terror of snakes and a brown Virgin's eyes.

But remembering it all now, she'd become a doctor not to help others but to cure her helplessness . . . to cure her guilt at not being able to save her mother. Her mother never should've died. People *were* complicated. Ten years old, screaming and crying, massaging her mother's chest, blowing air into her mouth, trying to do the CPR she'd seen on TV. Ultimately, the only power she had was to sit, hold her mother's hand, and watch over her still body. Day became night, night, day, then night again. Then, the cycle began again. Only when a disgruntled chauffeur came to see why the maid wasn't cleaning his mistress's home did the police come and drag her, kicking and screaming, away.

Thinking about her mother, Marie—the murdered girl, Marie-Claire, thinking about herself, another plain Marie—she knew she'd have to name her baby girl Marie-Claire. After her mother.

Like mother, like daughter. *Four Maries.*

Surely, this was fate.

* * *

"Heh, Almost-Doctor."

"Heh, Sully."

"Got a good dog here."

Kind Dog, tail wagging, limped out of Sully's cubicle, rounding the corner with a grin.

Marie felt her spirits lift. She stooped, rubbing the dog's ears. "I missed you."

The dog licked her cheek.

It was true. Seeing the dog made her feel she had a defense against loneliness.

"I'll keep him any time you want."

"He's sweet, isn't he?"

"Likes my harmonica music."

"Did he sing?"

"A few howls. Took his solo like a pro."

"Come on, Kind Dog." He hopped beside her, out the door, into the damp night air. She reached into her purse for keys. Damn. She'd done it again. Forgotten she was without a car.

Two bright lights rounded the corner. "Here." Reneaux, from the inside, pushed open the door. Before she could say anything, Kind Dog scooted into the car and leaped onto the backseat.

"Come on. Your car's been dusted for prints. It's with a friend of mine. It'll be as good as new tomorrow."

Marie felt reluctant, didn't want to keep being beholden to Reneaux. "DuLac said his home wasn't far. I can walk."

"Your dog can't."

Marie looked at Kind Dog, his head out the window, his tongue lolling.

"Thanks again."

Kind Dog pushed his head between two bucket seats, his teeth nipping at a white package.

"What's in the bag?"

"Marrow bones. Beef ribs. Thought Dog might like it for dinner."

"Cooked or raw?"

"Gonna be cooked," said Reneaux, lifting the bag away from Kind Dog. "DuLac's boiling the water. Making a stew."

Kind Dog barked. Marie couldn't help but laugh.

DuLac's home surprised her. It was serene, elegant, filled with French antiques.

"La Belle Epoque," he said. He was dressed in a velvet smoking jacket; no doctor whites.

"What?"

"Paris, 1900s. Turn of the century. But the era started long before that—the mid-1800s. America was still in the throes of slavery, cotton, and gin. Proust was writing *Remembrance of Things Past*. Saint-Saëns and Fauré were making music to "awaken in us the mysterious depths of our soul." Massenet was creating *Thaïs*, his great opera about a tortured monk falling in love with a prostitute. The monk becomes a madman; the prostitute becomes a saint. Irony. Sophistication, *non*? The French know about life and love."

"Listen." He pressed the CD button. A baritone soared; the melancholy was invasive. Marie felt uneasy. The warm tones ended in a scream.

El came out of the kitchen. "Just give me blues." She hugged Marie, patted Kind Dog. She hugged Reneaux, too. Marie felt jealous of their easy friendship.

"Eat. Eat." DuLac gripped her hand. "No business 'til after dinner. Right, Reneaux?"

"Right. Just lead me to the food."

DuLac slid open the dining room doors. It was breathtaking. French linens, candelabras on the table, plush velour chairs. There was gold flatware, gold-trimmed china. Napkins tied with ribbons. Sparkling Waterford crystal. A centerpiece of flowers: freesia with white calla lilies. The scent was heady, overpowering.

A chandelier and candelabra held red, beeswax candles. On the walls were paintings of nudes: cream-colored women lounging in boudoirs; a voluptuous blonde standing boldly under a tree; nymphs cavorting by a stream. On the fourth wall was a huge gilt-trimmed mirror, echoing the image of the table, the decadent nudes, and Marie, standing at the table's center. Reneaux looked at her, amused.

El scowled. "Looks like a brothel, don't it?"

"El's just jealous of my good taste." DuLac set down his first gold-plated bowl of food: gumbo, thick with okra and rice; next, collard greens with fatback, black-eyed peas, then platters of cornbread and yams.

"Slave food. On nineteenth-century French plate," DuLac snorted, delighted. "The wine is Château Lafite. A rare bottle for a rare evening. No moonshine. Eat. Eat. Drink."

"When'd you have time to cook, DuLac?"

"I always have good food waiting. My table set." He grinned, and Marie saw not the half-drunk, cynical doctor but a generous man, expansive with hospitality and fellowship.

She murmured, "I'm starved," and dug into the best food she'd ever tasted.

Kind Dog gnawed on bones.

Between bites, Reneaux, El, and DuLac teased one another. All old friends. Her mama would have liked this. Liked them. Reneaux was in middle school when DuLac and El were in high school.

"He was bad," chortled El.

"Full of trouble," echoed DuLac.

"Don't be telling tales on me."

"Reneaux was the trouble man, gangster then, Marie. Always tearing up screens, throwing balls through windows. Even stole penny candy from the corner store."

"I did not."

"Did, too. You were best at hustling. Playing sax in the Quarter."

"I didn't know you played," said Marie.

"Lots you don't know," said DuLac.

Reneaux laughed. "Some days I made ten bucks."

"On your raggedy-ass music?"

"No, the boy's music is good," El defended. "Sometimes, though, not enough soul. Flat improvisations."

"Y'all watch out now. I'll have to arrest you for disrespecting an officer."

"I'm scared," said DuLac. "So scared I think I'll get dessert."

"I'll help," said El, picking up dishes. Marie stood. El winked. "I can handle this, Marie. You and Reneaux stay here. Relax."

"They seem like an old married couple, don't they?" asked Reneaux. "I'm not sure but DuLac may have asked El to marry him. They went to high school together. He's a good six years younger. El was a backwoods girl. She lied about her age to get an education. She looked young even then."

"Did she lie about you? About your childhood?"

"Naw. All her tales about me are true. I was a punk but I played good music."

Marie smiled. She liked this man.

"Here 'tis. Pièce de résistance."

El carried the bowls of ice cream. DuLac poured rum over the sautéed bananas and lit it with a candlestick. Blue flames leaped upward. "Maman Marie." DuLac scooped the bananas over ice cream.

Marie cleaned her bowl like a starving girl. Reneaux let Kind Dog lick his spoon. El had two servings. Reneaux, three. DuLac smiled, pleased with himself. His spoon slowly stirring a café au lait.

"Now. Brandy."

Marie groaned. She was satiated.

"Its customary. Tell her, Reneaux."

"He does love his rituals, Doc."

"Brandy after every meal. Including breakfast," quipped El.

"I'll light the fire."

"Isn't it too hot?" asked Marie.

"Never. Where's your romance? Adventure?"

Reneaux sat on a pillow on the floor. Marie joined him. Kind Dog rested his head in her lap. El complained about her bad back and chose a chair.

DuLac brought brandy swirling in crystal. "VSOP. My finest."

Marie felt pleasant, no, more than that—this was the nicest evening she'd ever had in New Orleans or anywhere. DuLac, who rarely smiled, seemed happy. El looked regal in her straight-back chair. Reneaux looked desirable, the flames highlighting the contours of his face. Still, he stared into the flames like there was something there to find.

Five minutes. Maybe ten. Soothing fellowship—a moment when all seemed right with the world.

Then, Reneaux sighed, reaching in his jacket for his notepad. "This is what I know." His intonations were clipped.

El perched forward. DuLac clasped his hands, his chin resting on the steeple of fingers. Marie shook her head, trying to focus. She'd have an aching head tomorrow. She set her empty glass on the fire grate.

"The girl found today. No name yet. All the girls were pregnant. Innocents."

"How innocent can they be if they were pregnant? With no wedding rings?"

Marie was surprised by El's question—it was mean-spirited.

DuLac shrugged. "Two high-school girls. Runaways, maybe. All of them underage, like the DeLaCroix girl. None twenty-one. All of them had something not identified in their system."

"Like what?" Marie heard her voice slurring.

"That's it. We don't know. Something."

"Marie-Claire, too?"

"Don't know yet. Need the family's permission to disturb the tomb."

"They buried her?" asked DuLac.

Reneaux shook his head. "City charity. But since we now know who she is, legally, we need the family's permission."

Hands trembling, Marie wiped sweat from her brow.

"We're still investigating the connection to Jacques Paris. He might've known the first girl—they went to high school together. On the other hand, Jacques was known to pick up women."

114

"I'm not embarrassed, Reneaux."

"Some say he wasn't too particular. I mean, he just seemed to love women. Didn't matter whether they were young or old, fat or slim. Everyone agrees he enjoyed women." Reneaux cleared his throat.

"That's a good thing, isn't it?" asked Marie. "Liking women?"

"Yeah. Good thing," said Reneaux. "Real good thing." He cleared his throat again. "Jacques died of an overdose. Massive infusion of heroin."

"He died in Breezy's. The back room," said Marie.

"How do you know this?" asked DuLac.

Marie shrugged. Her tongue felt thick in her mouth.

Reneaux jotted notes. "I'll get a search warrant."

"We've also lifted prints from Marie's car. Thugs. A man named Arnaud, wanted for armed robbery. Assault with a deadly weapon. The others, petty thievery. Handles like Hammer, Reggae, and Pip."

DuLac, his elbows on his knees, swirled the brandy in his glass. "Two women thrown at Charity's door. Killed elsewhere, dropped in Emergency. Think my hospital is a trash dump? Folks dying every day. Murdered. Car accidents. Suicides. Not sick, just dead. Some fool killing women and dumping them like trash."

"How do you know it's one person?"

"What you mean?" asked El.

"I mean, how does DuLac know it's one person?" murmured Marie. "Maybe it's people? People wanting women murdered."

"Maybe the unidentified substance had something to do with it," said Reneaux.

"That's stretching—don't you think?" DuLac was insistent, probing. "Substance or not, the dead can't be revived."

Marie shuddered. Without asking, DuLac, bending on one knee, poured more brandy into her glass.

"He's been known to hit women," murmured El.

"Who?" Marie asked.

"Allez. No charges pressed. He's clean," said Reneaux.

"'Clean as dirt,' my mother would say," snapped El.

"Let's not get into what mamas would say—mine could outtalk you, outwit you any day," said DuLac.

"What she say?" cooed El.

"She say—" DuLac whispered into El's ear.

El laughed. Harsh. DuLac joined her, and Marie thought, for a minute, they looked like drunken hyenas.

DuLac poured more brandy into everyone's glass.

"Still I think it's strange. Allez showing up today of all days."

DuLac's finger drummed on the overstuffed chair. A simple tap of his index finger, then the beat became syncopated. Index finger alternating with thumb.

The beat was soft. Marie wasn't sure anyone else heard it.

The fire hissed, twisting smoke into chords.

"My mama used to say, 'Bad men always good-looking. Evil likes a pretty face.'"

"Then I must be Satan," hiccuped Reneaux.

"Hah," DuLac laughed. "My mama say, 'What goes around, comes around.'"

"Your mama's dead." El stamped her white nurse's shoe.

They must be drunk, Marie thought. Me, too. Her head and limbs heavy, she felt like she was weighted, ready to slide to the ground. DuLac's fingers tapped a rhythm and she felt her soul responding.

"*Marie.*" *Someone called her name.* She looked up.

Above the fireplace was a painting. Thick, dark colors: a brick church; night sky; black wrought iron. Even a flock of crows diving, swooping along the horizon. Black and brown figures were dressed in white. It was some kind of ceremony. A woman was in the center, a snake wrapped about her arm.

She could hear her mother: "This is the snake. Damballah-wedo."

She was young. Three, maybe four.

The woman in the painting was dancing, her hips swaying.

Mother was pointing at the crucifix. "Say, 'Goodbye,' Marie. Say, 'Goodbye.'" Mother kissed Christ's feet and the snake. She stuffed the crucifix with its dangling beads into a velvet bag.

Marie shivered. She was drunk. They were all drunk. She looked above the fireplace.

The painting's colors seemed to brighten, then fade. Brighten, then fade.

Think. Like a doctor. She'd been drunk before. Even with Jacques, she hadn't felt this lethargy. She knew how to hold liquor. Tonight: two glasses of wine; two glasses of brandy. An overheated room. Yes. Drunk? Yes. Unsafe to drive? Yes. Her mobility impaired.

But something else stirred in her blood.

She felt hypersensitive. Preternaturally keen. She could smell sweet musk on Reneaux, see sweat rising along his brow. El scratched her neck, her nails causing small tremors of follicles and skin. DuLac's heart beat—blood rushing in, blood rushing out—keeping time with his finger tapping out a rhythm with the strength of a bass drum.

The painting was alive.

She looked at DuLac. His lids heavy, she knew, nonetheless, he was watching her.

El was humming, moaning, "Yes, Lord. Yes, Lord." Like they were in church. Marie could see capillaries pinking El's cheeks, brightening her eyes. "My mama was the best."

Reneaux was pretending to play the sax.

Think. She'd been drugged. They'd all been.

Fear overwhelmed her. What did she really know about El, DuLac, and Reneaux?

Her weight shifted, she leaned to the right, then, slowly, fell. Her head on the carpet, Kind Dog licked her face.

Reneaux was shouting but she couldn't hear him. Then, she heard, "Name? What's your name?"

Words wouldn't come out of her mouth.

"Yes, Lord. Yes, yes, Lord." El was on her feet, stamping a rhythm. DuLac's hands were pounding the chair, his chest, thighs—everything had become a drum.

Marie jerked toward the grate. The fire was singing, calling out her name. *Marie.* Flames leaped, expanding with air, licking the chimney sides, darting toward the room's heart.

"What's your name?" Reneaux slurred. "Name?"

"Je suis Marie." *But it wasn't her voice. It was lower, more timbre.*

"Bathroom, I need to go. Get up." Reneaux tried to steady her, but they both tripped. Kind Dog yelped, scooted up, his tail wagging.

She felt like she was in the fun house. The floor rose, making waves, like a distorted carnival mirror. El was still shouting. She'd gone on to Jesus. Calling his name. "Lord. Precious Lord."

DuLac was chanting a work song: "Heh, yah, heh, yah. Lift that bale . . ."

She felt scared. Panicked. She stumbled forward.

"Turn left," Reneaux called. "The other way. Other way."

El's laughter wafted behind her.

She inched down the hall. Her stomach roiling, her hands flat against the wall, feeling her way as if she was blind.

On the left was a door. Painted with layers of red. Almost lacquered.

Her hands touched the smooth grain. *The door seemed alive, the air surrounding it, different, filled with the promise . . . of what?*

She looked, side to side. The hall seemed endless. *A haunting infinity. The only escape was through the door.* Her hand turned the knob.

She stepped inside.

* * *

There was an altar, lit with candles, a tin plate filled with dried fruit (raisins, dates, pomegranates) and seeds (sunflower, corn, wheat). There was a rosary, a dried snakeskin, and a small drum (a *djembe;* she'd seen one in an African history book). Above the altar was a painting. The same painting she'd seen in the living room, but somehow different. *More alive,* she thought. But that didn't make sense.

She stepped closer.

The world captured in the gilt frame invited her in.

Night. A raging bonfire. Specks of crimson rose into the gray-

midnight-blue sky. Figures in white formed a circle, swaying. All watched the woman in the center, dressed in an indigo skirt streaked with gold. A snake curled about her arm, its head resting against her shoulder.

Marie inched closer. *On the far left were drummers: some, their hands poised above drums, others, their hands hitting against their bare chests. Everyone's face seemed ecstatic; only the woman in the center seemed composed—cynical, her brows arched.*

Small groups of people stood, mingling, watching the dancers, swaying, circling. The lovely woman trapped in the middle.

Church spirals peaked in the background. A gull hovered over the roof, distressed and off course. Rats skittered in the side alley, tearing at some kind of flesh. A lone carriage was rounding the bend.

Marie knew this place—Cathedral Square. In the French Quarter off Pierre Antoine Alley. Right across from the Mississippi River and the Riverwalk where steamboats took tourists up and down the river. Every day of the week, the lawn in the middle of the square was filled with drunks, lovers, tarot card mystics, and trinket peddlers. Saturdays and Sundays, wedding parties posed for pictures, accompanied by musicians straight from Preservation Hall; other times, magicians did tricks, making doves appear and coins disappear for tourist dollars. Cathedral Square was always noisy, bustling, wide awake even on a Sunday dawn, with tourists gulping beer in plastic cups, hustlers trying to make a living on pity and souvenirs.

Except, in the painting, it was Cathedral Square from long ago. The 1800s. A blend of cultures: African slaves, Spanish aristocrats, American sailors, and French nuns, the Sisters of Ursuline, dressed in black wool robes.

Horse-drawn carriages still carted lovers about the square, but the carriage in the painting was no tourist contraption—*instead, it was a regal closed carriage with a black-suited driver, and a gas lamp perched on the roof's edge. Inside, Marie could see a man in a top hat; the veiled face of a woman leaning out the window, craning to see the dancers.*

Many of the bystanders wore coarse cotton but others in the crowd of black, brown, and white people were dressed in silk and linen, with boots and satin shoes instead of bare feet. All watched the woman in the center of the circle, among the still swirl of dancers.

Marie studied the bottom right corner. ML 1873. An artist's scrawl.

Out of the corner of her eye, Marie saw movement.

She stared at the painting—great swashes of color, a crowd scene painted in detail, each character unique. Some, yearning, some mesmerized; some laughing; some, their faces wrinkled with outrage; some, making the sign of the cross; some, hands upraised, looking into the darkening sky. A dog nipped at a man's boot; a pickpocket let his hand slide into a bystander's pocket; a prostitute offered her body for coins. Rich and poor, young and old, black, white, and in between, had come to see the amber-colored woman in the square.

Marie needed to get to the bathroom. She needed to rinse her mouth and face, stop her hallucinations.

A dancer's arm moved. Then another dancer's arm, then another and another. Then an arm, a foot, the tilting of a head, the thrust of hips. The woman in the center swayed, then turned to the right, slowly at first, then faster and faster until she was a spinning whirl of brown, indigo, and gold.

Marie shook herself. She was ill. She needed to go home, rest. Her hands clutched the gilt frame.

She heard drums. The same rhythm DuLac had tapped on his chair. *Men and women were echoing the rhythm with their feet, a syncopated, almost frenetic beat. Only the woman in the center seemed beyond rhythm, whirling with a passion—for what? Of what? Possession?*

Marie smelled fish, fire smoke, the Mississippi sluggish with algae. She smelled bodies, rank with sweat, curiosity, and fear.

The carriage had moved across and out of the scene. The drummer's hands were a flurry of pounding. A young boy was crying; a man had cracked his pipe flute.

Upstage, in the far right, a tall man stepped into the scene. Kingly, dressed in a billowy white shirt and white pants; his left hand dangled a chicken, its neck twisted and snapped.

The man walked forward, measured, stately, until he was slightly behind the dancers. Behind the woman. He glared at the scene—at her—with hatred.

Down left, a small man held a drum between his knees. A bucket was beside him. The darkness inside the bucket began moving, distinct threads, garter snakes writhing over one another, over the bucket's edge.

The woman stopped spinning, her back toward the ground; her face, toward the man. The man stepped forward. The snake reared its head. The man stopped. The dancers stopped. Only the drums kept luring.

The woman turned face forward, staring directly outward from the frame, at Marie, and smiled.

Marie screamed.

DuLac was holding her up, his arms about her waist, his mouth close to her ear.

"You were there. Cathedral Square."

"No."

"1873. Marie Laveau, the height of her powers. You were there."

"No."

"Leave her alone, DuLac." It was Reneaux. "You've done enough harm."

"Harm?"

DuLac clutched her tighter and Marie could smell the same curiosity and fear, the same rancid sweat as in the painting.

"*Alors*, she needs to know who she be."

"No," Marie screamed, twisting from his grasp.

"Let her be." Reneaux was beside DuLac, his hand inside his jacket, on his gun.

El was weeping in the corner. A pink rosary pressed to her lips.

"It's her," said DuLac.

"You're out of your mind," snapped Reneaux.

"It's you."

"No," said Marie, stumbling. Her hand touched the paint. It was warm—the oil seemed liquid. But the figures were still—no movement, no sound, no smells.

The woman in the center was in a new position. Hands folded, head bowed, she stood forlorn within the crowd's heart. The snake was wrapped about her waist. A black pearl rosary dangled over her arm.

The painting was no longer a replica of the painting in the living room, over the fireplace. This painting had changed from an exuberant ritual to a somber, sinister dance. *The man was threatening; the woman waited for the blow.*

Allez. The man looked like Allez. The woman looked like her.

The painting changed again. The woman was her mother. Her. Someone else. Then, her again. The man, always the same. Allez. Allez threatening her mother, her ancestor.

Upstage, in the dark shadow of the cathedral, a wooden door opened. A girl, in a chignon, held hands with a younger girl. Both resembled her. The younger girl held a baby upside down.

Inhale, exhale. Inhale, exhale. Calm. Marie needed to think . . . needed to understand the painting's clues. Needed to know why she hallucinated, why she saw herself steeped in an outrageous world.

Time slowed.

Marie looked at El. Her mascara streaked, she was forlorn and ancient. Reneaux was intense, coiled, watching DuLac.

DuLac, palms open, shrugged. "You were there, Marie," he whispered. "Think. Didn't your mother give you something? A reminder that you were there."

DuLac was no longer the world-weary doctor. He was certain, self-assured. "Remember? You were there." *He reached out, his hand transformed into a snake.*

Marie screamed, turned and ran. She heard Reneaux calling her. Still she ran, down the hall, through the living room.

"Marie," Reneaux shouted.

She didn't care about remembering. Didn't care about ceremonies in Cathedral Square. Didn't care about a painting that seemed to hold life within its frame. Still, she looked—at the painting above the fireplace. This painting was a celebration, an ecstatic dream.

She ran.

Kind Dog barked. "Stay," she shouted. "Stay."

Onto the porch, down the front steps, she ran. Ran along darkened streets, ran and ran . . . until her lungs ached, until she was lost.

She dodged into an alley, wandered into backyards, all the time hearing, "Marie!" El's high-pitched screech, haunting. "Marie." DuLac's quiet voice wrapped inside her head.

She kept running, her heart pounding, pumping blood, in and out, in and out. *She ran and found herself inside her dream. A mist enveloping her.*

She was a child again. A runaway from foster care, knowing in a matter of seconds, she couldn't stay where Social Services had left her. Couldn't stay in a home without her mother. Couldn't stay in a home that smelled of lye and alcohol, soiled diapers and Sloppy Joe's. She'd been caught, beaten, locked in her room, but tonight, she'd outrace hell if she had to.

Time to be hard again, not gullible, seduced by false kindness. El, DuLac, Reneaux were her enemies. Manipulating. Wanting something from her.

Tough. She'd survived by being tough; she'd win the baby back by being tough. Then she wouldn't be lonely. Alone again. "Dig down deep," she thought. Find the hard little girl. The one whose mother was dead. The one who'd scrimped for college, ignoring those who'd said she'd fail. The one who made it through med school, traveled to New Orleans on her own.

New Orleans—city of sin. City of Sin.

She stopped. The upside-down baby. Goat without horns. She knew, without knowing how she knew, that the baby was intended as a sacrifice. Save the child and she'd save herself.

But how were the murdered women connected?

"Mother?"

She felt a sweet wisp along her spine. She'd been lured to Orleans. It'd been her mother who'd kept her history hidden. It was her mother who now wanted her here.

Beneath a lamppost was a man in black hat, tuxedo, and white gloves. A rose in his front pocket. He smiled. She walked past him only to see two others, standing behind him like mirror images. In unison, they lifted their hats and bowed their heads.

Marie heard drums, like a pied piper, luring her. The men in hat and tails followed. Menacing yet not. Human yet not. Alive, yet not alive.

She shook her head. The chemical—herb? root? whatever it was—had been in her system, how long? An hour? Two? How long before it wore off? She knew she had to move forward, go on—*do* something. She'd come to New Orleans for some purpose. *She followed the men in top hat and tails.*

Rats rattled trash cans. Men harmonized on street corners Some stared at her—some mocking, some grinning, salacious, at a woman alone.

She'd turned south instead of north. She wanted to hail a cab, board a bus . . . but her feet kept moving, the streets growing more deserted, the moon rising higher, higher, then beginning its downward crest. Bright yellow. Stars like diamonds. She couldn't stop if she wanted to.

On and on she went, until she recognized Breezy's. Low-slung shack. A squashed beetle. Music, bass-driven and raunchy. Cars parked everywhere. Men in jeans, women in tight skirts loitered outside. Inside, a mystery; nothing to see behind the closed door and blackened windows.

Why was she here?

The men in top hat and tails had disappeared. It was just her, hiding beneath the branches of a willow, her body leaning against bark to keep from sliding down to the ground. She kept staring at the building, thinking of the wizened woman inside who disowned her granddaughter and great-grandchild.

Marie blinked.

The building's weathered lines faded, like a photo undeveloping itself, slipping back in time. The building was freshly whitewashed. Distinct on the dark horizon. Tea roses flourished beneath the windows. Women—black, yellow, and brown—were entering the front door, which was wood, not steel. Some wore flowers in their hair to match their silk pastel skirts; others wore head wraps, and aprons with wide sashes. Some carried lamps; some, buckets of water for the evening wash. Some walked stiffly; others dragged tired feet. Paler women, dusted with bronze, stepped delicately down from carriages, black menservants lighting their way.

A white man from one of the carriages shouted, "Cher. Cher."

One of the women giggled and waved a fan. Another screamed, "Pig. Bastard," while adjusting her bodice.

Horses snorted, pawed the ground.

Someone tossed gold coins from a carriage window. All the women ignored the sparkling gold in the dirt.

There was a scream. Marie rushed forward. *Another scream, muffled from inside the house.* Marie stopped: two groups of revelers, from two centuries, were staring at her. Women in leather pants, high heels, and hair extensions. *Women in ball gowns, satin slippers, their hair in French twists with flowers. She heard another scream.*

One of the ghosts touched her; Marie shivered.

"He's coming."

She saw Marie-Claire.

"Run," said another, and Marie turned her head to the left and saw the girl from the ambulance, her face woeful.

"Run."

"Run, run, run . . ." a dissonant chorus. "Run," screamed a girl with a hoop ring pierced through her eyebrow.

A bouncer moved toward her.

"Marie." It was Reneaux, pulling her back behind the tree.

The scene disappeared.

"I saw them. I know I saw them."

"Who?"

"The girls who were murdered. They were here, dressed like queens."

She pulled back, remembering who was holding her. "Let me go, Reneaux. Why should I trust you?"

"Because I'm here." He held her steady, his hands on her waist. "Not with DuLac."

"How'd you know where I'd be?"

"Dog. He's safe. In the car."

Marie slumped against his chest. "I'm ill, Reneaux. Seeing things."

"I know." He stroked her hair.

"DuLac drugged me."

"All of us. But you're the most affected."

Willow threads made bars of shadows. With her fingers, she touched Reneaux's lips, tracing their softness. She crossed her arms over her belly. A grinding, pulsating love song wafted from the house. There weren't any screams. Only laughter. Lustful cat-calls.

"I don't know what's wrong with me."

She wanted some comfort, some tangible reality. How to explain that to Reneaux?

"Hide." Reneaux pressed her against the tree, his body covering hers, the two of them merging into wood.

Two black town cars pulled up. Stragglers, outside the shack, dispersed or went inside. From the first car, three men stepped out. Tall, broad, announcing by their stance that they were bodyguards. Men packing weapons. Men who didn't mind causing harm. Knives, fists, bricks. No matter.

At the second car, the slim driver, subservient, hat in hand, opened the passenger door. Allez stepped out.

Reneaux murmured, "Hush, Marie. *Ma petite,* keep still."

Allez looked straight at the tree. Marie didn't breathe. Nor did Reneaux. The willow branches were like gauze curtains.

Marie, looking through the weeping branches, swore the house was freshly white again . . . and Allez was dressed in no dark, conservative suit but in drawstring white pants, a white shirt, billowing about his collar and cuffs. He was the man inside the painting.

Her body went rigid and Reneaux whispered, "Ssssh, ssssh," and pressed his lips against her ear.

Allez cocked his head. Marie felt he was looking straight at her. Powerful. Royal. Odd to think that—but there he was—a black man looking for all the world like he was a king. He smiled at Marie. She was sure of it.

He shouted gaily, "*Vite. Vite.* Let's go inside. See what riches are in store."

One of the guards laughed, then swallowed his laughter when Allez turned his head in his direction. Two guards moved first, fronting for their master, entering the shack without knocking. The chauffeur, shoulders rounded, lit a cigarette. The third guard walked the perimeter, alert for any danger.

"We need to leave. I don't want to confront Allez without backup."

They moved slowly. Step by step. Inch by inch.

Marie had stepped backward through time. Space. She'd done that. Surely she could step quietly across dirt, cracked asphalt so she and Reneaux were neither seen nor heard.

Their lives depended upon it.

If nothing else, she knew that. Knew it as surely as . . .

. . . *she knew her mother's spirit was still alive. Knew the murdered girls were linked to the past.*

* * *

Kind Dog was waiting in the car. He didn't bark—almost as if he knew the need for secrecy. He sniffed Marie, tried to lick her cheek. Reneaux put his Cadillac in neutral, relying on gravity to pull his car forward over gravel. Then, once he was on the street, he turned the engine over, gunned the gas, and set the headlights on high.

"Haven't we done this before?" Marie murmured.

* * *

Marie's head lolled back on the seat. She felt herself, yet not her-self. Something had surely happened. New Orleans had added another dimension to her. Or had it been there all along?

"Why do you think he did it?"

"DuLac? He's a mixed-up soul. But I'm sure he thought he was helping."

She could see DuLac's eyes, too bright and stunned. Hear his words, "You were there, Marie. You were there." Where? Cathe-dral Square? A figure inside a painting?

"What'd he give us?"

"I don't know. But he gave it to all of us to avert suspicion. Including himself. I decked him after you left."

Marie could see DuLac, lips bloodied, on the floor, muttering, "It helps the loas to come."

"What are *loas?*"

"Where'd you hear that word from?"

"DuLac. He's murmuring it now."

"You're scaring me."

"The light's green."

The car lurched forward.

Legba, remove the barrier so I may pass through.
Remove the barrier so I may visit the *loas.*

DuLac, sitting in a stupor, cradled his head in his hands.

Marie watched the street gliding by—neon streaking color across the skyline, women dangling scarves from balconies, an old woman pushing an airport cart stuffed with lawn bags.

There were strains of music, too—blues, zydeco, Preservation

Hall jazz, rock, even disco. Nighttime in New Orleans was like nowhere else—its own season of darkness that wouldn't stay dark (neon, candles, artificial gas lamps, strobe lights), a darkness that roared, releasing inhibitions. Thousands strolled, danced, stumbled and fell on ancient cobblestone; some clutched lovers, others, plastic cups of beer, some flicked cigarette ashes; others grabbed at their crotch. Men urinated on patches of grass. Prostitutes wet their tops, their nipples outlined, rigid in the night air. Above the bars were rooms with cheap curtains and silhouette figures touching, parting, then touching some more.

Sin season. Lust. Greed. Gluttony. Sloth.

Funny, she realized she wasn't angry any longer at DuLac. Anger—another sin. She felt depleted. Used up; her body starved. Calcium leeching from her bones, muscle breaking down, her womb's eggs decomposing. Almost as if she could feel her body dying.

But she'd seen something special. Felt special. Each day she'd been in New Orleans—she'd felt she'd been changing, experiencing unsettling dreams, talking ghosts, honeysuckle flowers triggering memories, and now this "sight"—"waking dreams"—she didn't know what to call it. She only knew she could see beyond seeing.

A car's headlight whizzed by. A misty drizzle. Reneaux clicked on the windshield wipers. One swipe, there was modern New Orleans. *Next swipe, there were shadow images. Horse-drawn carriages instead of cars. Slaves instead of equal citizens.* Twenty-first century versus the nineteenth.

"Are you okay, Marie? I mean, Doc. Doctor Levant."

She looked over at Reneaux's profile. He was handsome, fit for an Egyptian coin.

"Marie's fine."

He looked away from the road. "You sure?"

"I'm sure."

He smiled and tapped the gas lightly. "I'll have you home in no time."

Kind Dog scratched a paw to get out.

Reneaux opened the back door, turned off the headlights, then moved around the side of the car and opened the passenger door. He extended his hand. Marie didn't move.

"What's the matter?"

"Someone's up there." She was staring into her lap, her heart racing, more fearful then she'd ever felt.

"How do you know?"

"Just do."

Reneaux touched his gun, looking up at the apartment windows. "It's dark."

"Wait."

Moonlight filtered through the French doors.

"Nothing, Marie. Nothing's up there."

Kind Dog hopped back to the car, brushed against Reneaux.

"He's there."

"Who?"

"I don't know." Her eyes filled with tears. "Allez, I think."

"We just left him."

"There."

A shadow fell angular, elongated across the French doors. Someone was hiding, his back against the left wall.

"There's rumors that Allez, at any time, can be in more than one place."

"You believe that?"

"You?"

She looked up, blinking back tears, biting the inside of her cheek. She needed to be hard and harsh. "He's waiting for me."

Reneaux whistled low.

Kind Dog perked his ears, leaped into the car. Reneaux quietly shut the side doors. Then he slid into the driver's seat, released the brake and clutch, and gently, ever so gently, turned on the engine.

* * *

Reneaux's apartment was north of the Quarter. Closer to Pontchartrain Park. His three-story building surrounded a courtyard in disrepair. Ferns were overly abundant. A fountain gurgled over cracked tile. Griffins hung above the arches, their beady eyes watching the courtyard's four corners. A metal staircase was burnished red with rust.

"I live on the top floor." Reneaux scooped up Kind Dog, and Marie, holding on to the rail, followed them. At the top of the stairs, she looked down.

"Do you see them?"

"Who?"

"The funny men." *They were standing solemnly, waving their white-gloved hands.*

Reneaux crossed himself.

"What's that for?"

"I don't see anything, but you do. Spirits?"

"You mean devils?"

"Don't know. Do you?"

"No." She shook her head, peering over the banister. "Just strange men in hat and tails."

"The Death gods. The Guédé."

"Evil?"

"DuLac wouldn't say so."

Kind Dog barked.

The tallest spirit-man lifted his hat. The three disappeared.

"I need a drink."

"Haven't you had enough mind-altering substances for one night?"

Marie thought for a second. "No."

* * *

"My home. Small. Not fancy."

It looked like a man's home. A studio with dishes in the sink. Voodoo Daddy beer bottles on the table. The floor.

A yellow bug light dangled over a beanbag chair. There was a sofa with a leopard throw rug. A stereo, and CD cases, that towered from the floor to the ceiling.

"Sit. Relax." Reneaux was emptying ashtrays, putting clinking bottles in his recycle bin. Picking up stray underwear and shoes. In the far corner, near the French doors and courtyard-view balcony, was a bed—not quite a double, but larger than a twin.

Marie stretched out on the sofa. "When will the drug wear off?"

"'Two hours at most,' DuLac said."

"How long has it been?"

"Four. Nearly five. You still seeing things?"

Marie didn't answer. Kind Dog climbed onto the sofa, curled against her abdomen, laid his head and paws across her thighs.

Marie felt comforted. She squeezed her eyes tight. Inside Reneaux's apartment, she felt relief. No ghosts, haints. *Loas,* as Reneaux called them.

No honeysuckle here. Only a musk scent. Maybe a bit of mold. She opened her eyes. A philodendron was dying in the corner. Sheet music was strewn across the bed. A sax rested on the pillow. On the coffee table were art and literary works. Harlem Renaissance books. Novels by Hurston. Poetry by Hughes. Even the collected works of Dunbar.

"Here."

She took the scotch. (She wouldn't cry. She wouldn't remember Jacques.)

"Ssssh." Reneaux patted her hand. She started crying. Kind Dog licked her cheek. (Damn. Double damn.)

"You can have the bed, you know."

"I'm not ready to sleep."

"Afraid?"

"Yes."

Reneaux bent, took off her flat, rubber-soled white shoes. He massaged her toes.

Her foot curled. "I'm ticklish."

"I was hoping you were." He laid his jacket over her, pressed the glass to her mouth. "Drink."

He walked across the room, lifted and cradled his sax, blew a soft stream of air. A soothing A, then C, then A again . . . and then, a tune spun itself out, hovering on the ceiling, notes that

136

seemed to verge on a cry. There was something between the notes, the rests, the lines, which she couldn't quite hear.

She sipped the whiskey, letting herself relax. Her hand stroked Kind Dog's fur; her chin rested on her chest.

*　*　*

She could feel the sun, healing strips of light. She didn't want to open her eyes. She just wanted to lie where she was, the dog curled up at her feet, Reneaux's jacket a comfortable weight on her chest. She could hear a steamboat's boom and churn, smell the sluggish Mississippi and naval oil.

She felt hungover. Mouth dry; eyes dry; skin taut. She must've fallen asleep on the couch. Last thing Reneaux had said was, "Let the music soothe you," and it had.

Reneaux was shuffling in the small kitchen, trying not to clang but clanging pots anyway, humming the sax melody to "God Bless the Child," then, crooning softly, "Your momma may have, your papa may have . . ." before diving back into a hum, blowing air between his lips in high, thin strips.

Lying on her couch bed, Marie could almost imagine her mother in the kitchen, singing like Reneaux, but her mother's songs were always mournful. Even when she was singing "good news" songs about heaven, paradise, and Jesus rising, there was melancholy.

Eyes still closed, Marie wished she were elsewhere. But where? Wherever she went, she'd still have to admit she could see spirits, ghosts. In dreams. Wide awake.

Reneaux pressed down the toaster spring. She smelled bread and could almost see stacks of toast glistening with strawberry jam.

Like once upon a time.

Where'd that come from?

A man had visited their apartment. Mother had let him sleep on the couch. She'd tried to stay awake, her ear pressed to the door, trying to hear the grown-ups speak. When she woke, she was tucked in bed and the man was whistling in the kitchen, making breakfast. For days, he cooked for her and her mother. Did chores. Took out trash. Cleaned. Stuffed shelves and refrigerator with food. Helped wash her doll's hair. Took her for rides perched high on his shoulders.

Then, he left. No explanation. No goodbye. For months afterward, she'd tormented her mother. "Where's Pa? Where's my papa?" She kept asking, as selfish as only a child could be.

Her mother spent weeks in bed. Like she'd given up—failed to see any need to take care of herself or her daughter now that the man wasn't there. Only when food, laundry gave out did her mother rise, swearing, "Never again."

She swore, making the sign of the cross, "I'll take care. Of my baby and me."

Not quite. Marie often took care of her—reminding her mother to dress warmly; eat. Even sleep when her mother would've tossed and cried all night. But her mother did go back to work, faithfully, scrubbing floors, ironing shirts, and dusting another family's portraits.

Later, at seven and eight, whenever she was angry with her mother, she'd ask, "Where's my papa?" Her mother grimaced. The argument ended and whatever it was she wanted, she got. An extra sweet. A new ribbon for her hair. Pennies for a comic.

But she despised the things she won. Feeling sorry, she'd pick flowers—dandelions sticking up through concrete, marigolds pushing through slats, or, if she was lucky, a rose, peeping above a fence. Her mother would kiss her and together, they'd play pick-up sticks—no mention of their fight. No mention of men—a man—in their life.

That's how it was. Just mother and child.

"Keep your head low." "Don't talk to strangers." Don't trust neighbors; don't make friends. Just her and her Maman. Yes. She'd called her that. When she was young. When they were alone. Creole had been her first language.

Why hadn't she remembered that?

"Speak Creole and the bogeyman will come."

When she forgot English and said, *"Fatiguée"; "J'desire lait,"* her mother would pinch her and she'd cry.

"Hush. Don't I take care of you? Don't I love you enough?"

She realized her mother had done the best she could.

As a child, she didn't understand why her mother was mean sometimes. Abrupt. Crying sad.

She'd only understood that to ask questions was to admit her mother lied, told tales, hid truths. Or, maybe, her mother was hiding from herself? It'd had nothing to do with Marie. The child. Everything to do with a broken woman. A single mother on her own.

* * *

Marie opened her eyes. Reneaux was standing over her.

"You okay?" he asked.

"Yeah."

"Sure?"

Reneaux's sympathy made her feel perverse. "How'd your brother die?"

Reneaux was still.

"I'm sorry. Bad habit. I think if I hurt you, I'll stop hurting."

Reneaux dropped to his knees. His hands covered Marie's; his face just inches from hers. Kind Dog turned his head, watching the two of them intent upon each other.

"Drugs—"

"No, don't tell me."

"I haven't spoken of it for fifteen years."

"Then don't. Not now. Madame wanted you to tell me. Means it's gonna hurt, doesn't it?" Marie caressed his ear, touched the crucifix dangling from his lobe. "I don't want you to be hurt."

Reneaux leaned forward. "DuLac says love is the real healer."

"Is that your pickup line? I'm sorry. I'm sorry." She grabbed his hand, wishing she could erase the hurt from his face. "Don't go. I've been eaten up ever since the baby's been gone." Ever since her mother died. The baby was pain twice over. Losses were mounting up.

Reneaux's face was a hair's breadth from hers. She could feel his uneven breath, feel the tenseness radiating down his back.

Kind Dog started whimpering.

"I'm sorry, I'm sorry." She pressed Reneaux's head to her heart.

"I murdered him." Reneaux whispered. Then she could feel the whirlwind gathering in his belly, coiling through his lungs, until it was a shrill howl flowing from his mouth.

She felt buffeted by his pain, pulled in by the undertow.

She tugged Reneaux, shifting his weight, pulling him up off

his knees to lie upon her. The two of them pressed into the sofa. Tight, cocooned together, shifting their weight against the cushions.

She understood the ferocity of pain. Understood how someone could howl like an animal. Then subside, hiding pain in sinews, bones, and blood. Year after year after year.

She felt the soft currents from his exhalations. She buried her face against his neck, kissed the soft flesh . . . then kissed again. She stroked his lower back, buttocks, the concavity between his waist and pelvis. She opened her mouth, biting into his shoulder. Teasing through cotton, nipping to get at skin. His breath more ragged; his body expressing its need, and hers, too, her inside, opening, unfolding, preparing for him.

Reneaux's head drew back. A question.

"Love heals. Isn't that what DuLac says?"

Love. As in solace, comfort, forgiveness. Christ's charity. All she'd ever had, all she ever thought she needed was sex.

Reneaux stood. She cried out, thinking he was leaving her. He neither wanted nor needed her. Then his arms slid under her shoulder and knees, and he lifted her like a babe. Lifted her and carried her to his bed.

"Love me," she pleaded, and he did.

* * *

Sweet, gentle loving. He gathered up the pieces of her and focused her on feeling. Slowly, a southern gentlemen, exploring her secrets—the skin behind her knees, the sensitivity of her nipples and breasts, the slope between her thighs. She wasn't sure he came. But she did, awash with feeling, her back arching, her entire being exalting.

She lifted her head to see Kind Dog sleeping, stretched full-length on the couch. She sighed, drifting in a haze of satiety, feeling for the first time that she'd found the path home.

Reneaux clutched her hands, stretching her arms outward, his fingertips opening her hands like she was pinioned to a cross. His head was beside her head, his body's weight pressing her deeper into the bed. His knees separated her legs, and he entered her body.

This time he took her down, deeper into herself. Aggressive. Intense. Working out his pain. Seeking forgiveness, pleasure-pain. She followed him. Matched his strokes. Let her loneliness touch his.

His arms encircled her. She rose; he shifted his weight onto his knees and heels. She rode him, quick, hard, her hands clasping his face, her tongue exploring his mouth. Then they were rocking together, moaning, matching each other's rhythm. On and on they rode, like they were being chased; their bodies locked, they were rushing to safety.

Their kiss, their rhythm, deepened. Her womb contracting, his penis thrusting, they swallowed each other's screams. His embrace hurt, her nails dug into his skin. They were both holding on for dear life. Holding, holding, riding to a horizon where they both gasped, their bodies shuddered, and feeling became light, turning into a spray of rainbows.

Their kisses became gentle. Eyes, nose, mouth, cheekbones, the hollow at the base of each other's throat, they kissed. Reneaux helped lower her onto the bed, his hands supporting her back. He stayed inside her. Their bodies were wet, sticky from semen and sweat. He murmured her name over and over.

"Marie, Marie, Marie. I adore, Marie." His teeth and tongue teased, nibbled her ear. She kept rubbing his shoulders, buttocks, and back.

Sweet yet not sweet.

Eyes closed, she didn't want to break the spell. Didn't want to see only fading lust in his eyes. Or denigrating manly triumph. Didn't want him to see how special his loving had been to her.

"Dream of me," he murmured.

She opened her eyes.

He was watching her. *Lovingly.* She hadn't known what that word meant between a man and a woman. *Lovingly*—how a parent watched a child. But between two consenting adults? *Lovingly.* That was how he was watching her and how she was watching him.

He drew out of her. She shifted sideways, one arm across his abdomen, his arm embracing her. She heard the slowing of his breath and heart, inhaled his scent mixed with hers. She sighed, closing her eyes, knowing he was watching over her.

Lovingly.

All day she slept, wrapped in a cocoon. Sheets twisted about her, sunshine warming her spirit.

She heard Reneaux tiptoeing, heard him take Kind Dog outside, heard him sitting by the edge of the bed, turning pages in a book.

She slept until evening matins, until the cacophony of bells began calling Catholics to prayer.

She could see the church. Same as in the painting. Allez was framed in the church door. Waiting for her.

She woke; Reneaux was sitting on the corner of the bed.

"It's Allez. He's behind everything."

"You sure?"

Holding the sheet to her breasts, she leaned forward and kissed Reneaux. "We should see DuLac."

"Sure?"

She laughed.

His palm cupped her face. Their eyes conveyed, if not exactly a vow of love, then a willingness to commit. "Sure?" he whispered.

His eyes somber, Reneaux was worried. Not about her, *for* her.

"Oui. Certainement."

His brows lifted. "You know French? Creole?"

"I'm discovering I know more than I think."

"That's good," he said, exaggerating his drawl.

She kissed his brow, nose, lips. "I've been hiding. Time to grow up. Discover who I am."

"Me, too," whispered Reneaux as he stroked her hair; they embraced and made love again.

ANOTHER BEGINNING

Two Thousand and Five

The only protection is . . . to see the self as other. Immortal.

Grandmère, my mother, my daughter, and myself—we were all named Marie.

This story is all of us.

Voodoo is worth passing on.

—Marie Laveau, June 12, 1881, early evening
(From Louis DeLavier's journal)

"You know me."

DuLac was slumped in a claw-footed chair, his head back and mouth half-open. Marie had asked Reneaux not to knock. Instead, they let themselves in, walking into the vestibule, its walls covered with velvet flocking. Marie was assailed by the home's hothouse scent, like entering another world, layered with incense, sweet flowers, and a hint of cinnamon. Excessive decadence. Eighty-eight degrees outside and the fireplace roared, flames licking the air.

An empty brandy glass, turned upside down, was next to DuLac's bare feet. He smelled of alcohol and dirty sweat. Shirt messed; belt buckle undone. Marie knew he hadn't been to work. There must've been comments in the ER today: "DuLac tied another one on"; "Drowned himself in the bottle"; "Gave himself an overdose." While she and Reneaux had found space to make love, DuLac had drunken himself into a stupor. And El? Knowing her, she'd be at work, fussing over patients, saying prayers to the Virgin and to wakeful spirits.

"You know me," Marie repeated.

"I knew your mother. And your mother's mother before."

Kind Dog nudged DuLac's knee.

DuLac stroked Dog's ears, then looked up at Marie, smiling, his face beatific. "You came back."

In that moment, Marie forgave him everything. She moved forward, watching his smile widen, his arms spreading wide. She fell to her knees, her head on his thighs, and he wrapped his torso over hers and held her, cradled her . . . and hummed.

"You?" she asked.

"*Oui,* I came to see you. In Chicago."

She looked at him, wistful.

"*Non.* I'm not your father. Just a man who tried to persuade your Maman to come home."

"You read my mind."

He smiled. "*Non.* Just your face. You'd the same look when you were a child. I don't think anyone knows who your father be. All I know is he terrified your Maman enough to run her off. Or, maybe, that's not right. Maybe someone terrified them both. She was so frightened."

"Too frightened."

"And what about you? Are you too frightened?"

"I'm scared but I feel as though I belong here. In New Orleans."

"*Oui.* You made it on your own. Found your way home. Eh, yé, yé, Maman Marie."

"Why do you call me that?"

"You think she's the one?" asked Reneaux, his voice overlapping Marie's.

DuLac laughed, high-pitched. "I need either an Aspirin or a drink."

"You'd better drink," said Reneaux. "Aspirin might kill you."

DuLac shrugged. He rubbed Kind Dog's head. Clutching the brandy bottle, his fat-bellied glass, he said, "Come with me," and led them down the hall.

"My chapel," he said, opening the door.

The room was dim, candles flickered, and incense, heady and sweet, burned in a gold cup. There was a statue of the Virgin, dressed in blue and white, a crucifix, and a charcoal drawing of an old man, back bent, with a walking stick.

"The Virgin, you know. Christ is always Christ. The old man is Legba. He's like St. Peter. He opens the gate to heaven, to the spirit world."

Marie stood on the threshold. DuLac was inside, before her; Reneaux, outside, behind her. Her breath came in quick bursts. If she stepped inside the chapel again, everything she knew would be transformed.

DuLac held out his hand.

Marie couldn't help thinking: "Why should I trust you?" But it wasn't really a matter of trust. She needed to go where DuLac could lead. She needed to be other than who she was—she hadn't been happy. Not since her mother died.

Still, she held back.

Reneaux whispered, "I'm here."

DuLac murmured, "I shouldn't have tricked you."

"No, you shouldn't have."

"I'm sorry." He edged closer. "I have loved you—always have. *Je t'adore.* I have loved you as a companion, a friend to the gods, my spirit adviser, my salvation, as my queen, down through the generations."

DuLac's fingers traced her cheekbones. "When you were a child, I loved you. Even when it was clear you had no idea of your legacy. I prayed for this day."

Love. As in charity? Christian charity? Or some perversion meant to steal away her soul? Did it matter?

She whose faith was untested, who prayed and believed in God because her mother had told her she ought to. But it'd been years since she'd been to Mass, never once in New Orleans, even though daily, the bells caroled and called. DuLac was encouraging blasphemy; yet, why did she feel such yearning? She didn't believe she was evil; rather, she was interested in love: Reneaux's love—she looked back at his clear, black face; DuLac's love—he believed in her when she didn't believe in herself.

A breath caressed her ear. Mother?

"She's here," said DuLac.

Marie stepped across the threshold.

"You'll find her in the painting."

Transfixed, Marie stepped closer and closer, smelling honeysuckle rising from the canvas.

"I don't understand."

"There's always a history. See." He pointed at the painting. "That's you."

"Me?"

"Your Maman, too. Blood ancestors."

"You're frightening me."

"*Non, ma petite.* Don't you feel memories? Snakes stirring in your blood?"

Marie felt awe. The scent was strong, buried in canvas and oil.

"Eh, yé, yé, Maman Marie. Eh, yé, yé," DuLac chanted. "Back through time. Twentieth century. Nineteenth. Eighteenth, seventeenth. For centuries, slaves were carted across the Atlantic. White Americans said, 'Slaves were blank slates.' They could write upon their souls.

"Not so. Slaves brought West African faiths. A belief in the power of the ancestors. In deities. A belief that the entire world was alive with spirits. Meaning—everyone and everything—needed respect, blessings. Here, in Louisiana, many of the slaves traveled from Africa to Haiti to here. The Code Noir required all slaves to be baptized Catholic. But their faith was *Voudon.* Voodoo, it was called in the New World. Their faith went underground, mixing and blending with Christianity. The Virgin Mary sometimes became Mistress Ezili. Or Aido-Wedo, a rainbow. Christ became kin to Damballah, the father to all the gods.

"Slaves went to church, confessed to priests for intercession with God. But they also kept alive their belief that if they called the gods themselves, the spirits would come. Despite distance, human cruelty, and suffering.

"Always a history, Marie. Look at the painting. A ceremony. Whites called it 'night dancing.' They thought blacks' dances were primitive, sensual, and barbaric. But these were the qualities of the masters. Pinched souls who couldn't see or understand a darker beauty. Who didn't understand that 'night dancing' was a ritual, a ceremony where humanity touched the divine.

"Always a history. Look, Marie."

It was her face.

"Women hand sight down through the generations."

"It isn't real."

"It is. The drug I gave you encouraged visions, but you've always had them."

"I'm not myself."

"You're more yourself than you've ever been."

Features shifted. "Mother?"

The face shimmered, changed again. It was her, yet not her. Mother, yet not. The eyes were black, penetrating. The small painted figure seemed suddenly larger than life. Her spirit overflowing the boundaries of canvas, dimension, time, and space.

"Generations of priestesses. All named Marie. Mixed bloods."

Marie swayed. Reneaux steadied her, and gave her a fleeting kiss. She looked at him in wonder. She wasn't used to men helping her, being touched by their goodwill. DuLac was shining with almost paternal pride. "Your gift takes many forms. Intuition—"

"Dreams?"

"*Oui.* Sometimes foresight. Prophecy. Sometimes, hindsight, mainly healing—"

"Then why couldn't I heal my mother?"

"Maybe she didn't want to be healed?"

"No." She looked at DuLac, then relented. "Yes, maybe." She didn't remember her mother's smiles or laughter, just her hard labor, tired body, and a depressed spirit.

"Your Maman ran from herself. Her history. Can't escape sight. Women hand sight down through the generations. See." His hand poked at the canvas. "See. Don't matter who the father be—sad but true. One, two, three Maries . . . never dying, circling, circling like the snake eating itself."

The dancers swayed. The snake twisted down Marie's arm.

"I know this place. Cathedral Square."

"Yes. If you call, the faithful will come again."

"2005—you'll have to get a permit," said Reneaux.

DuLac laughed. "Let's begin small. A ceremony here."

"When?"

"Now?"

"Tonight."

"I'm not sure."

"Search your heart. Tell me what you know."

Since she stepped on New Orleans soil, she'd been haunted. In her heart and soul, she knew more than she could account for—knew her dreaming was connected to the Maries. Baby made four. Knew she was connected to the women dying.

She peered closely at the world caught within the frame.

Where was the man?

* * *

Past midnight, the moon was high. Two matrons silently dressed her in white.

DuLac instructed: "We all wear white. For purity, cleansing. On white, the spirits paint their own colors. They paint the colors of the universe."

El arrived. Marie opened her arms and the two of them held on to each other for dear life.

"I'm sorry," moaned El. She looked as if she'd aged a dozen years.

"No need for sorry." Marie patted her back. "Ssssh." And as

she had with her Maman, Marie felt, for a moment, that she was the mother and El, the child.

"Time to begin," chortled DuLac.

Marie sat on a straight-back chair, her ankles and hands crossed. DuLac moved with the grace of a king. Through the front door, but mostly through the back, DuLac's small band of followers arrived. No more than a dozen. Marie wondered how many of them went to Mass on Sunday? But they were here now. "True believers," DuLac said. Mainly, they were old men and women—some gap-toothed, some rail-thin, some graying, others with hair white as cotton. One woman, Madame Yvonne, she'd seen for hypertension. She was lonely. Her children all lived North. She recognized "Petey," known for his binge drinking, sleeping on sidewalks. Erma, at least eighty, was called "Auntie" by everyone. Healed bone fractures were everywhere in her body—her arms, her legs, her ribs, her face. "Auntie" had been abused when she was young.

Another man, whom Marie didn't recognize, carried a flapping chicken. He stuffed the hen, squawking, into a wooden cage.

"Sacrifice," said DuLac. "The followers expect it. Afterward, I make gumbo."

It was surreal. A bad B movie.

Reneaux stood next to her, his hand on her shoulder, soothing.

Lastly, a boy entered, a buttery brown boy with thick black lashes and curly hair. A drum almost as tall as him hung from his shoulder. Marie thought he couldn't have been more than fourteen. He should've been in bed, making ready for a day of school.

"Without him, it wouldn't be complete," said DuLac. "He makes the call."

"Not you?"

DuLac shook his head. "Always the drum. The drummer calls the spirits. And when they come, they ride."

"Ride?"

"Possess."

She was scared again. Reneaux squeezed her hand.

The drum resounded. One hard beat. Then two. A call to attention. The followers' spines straightened, weary women became enlivened, men stepped in time, like martinets. The rhythm changed, cajoling in three-quarter time. Marie responded to the wooing, the rhythmic caress as the boy's hand swept across calfskins draped on wood.

The women and men, following DuLac's lead, swayed and chanted:

> Legba, remove the barrier for me
> So I may pass through
> Legba, remove the barrier for me
> So I may pass through to the spirit world.

The sound was like a round—voices overlapping, the drumming incessant and strong:

> Legba, remove the barrier for me
> So I may pass through to the spirit world.

The elderly men and women danced like youths, their faces aglow with pleasure. Aglow with an energy that seemed to wipe all cares, complaints, and life's losses away.

DuLac was majestic, awash with glory. He, too, looked younger.

If Marie didn't know better, she would've suspected them of being drugged. Or maybe this was a mass hallucination? Dispossessed people believing in something beyond themselves because they needed to believe. The disenfranchised trying to erase mortality and experience ecstatic joy.

DuLac opened the cage and held the chicken high. It was limp, resigned to its fate.

The drums grew louder; the dancers, more frenzied.

DuLac snapped the chicken's neck. Marie nearly screamed. DuLac used a surgical knife to cut the chicken's throat. Blood welled and dripped into a pan.

Marie felt nauseous. She wanted to run. But her legs felt leaden; she couldn't move.

Reneaux wasn't himself; he was staring at empty space, rocking forward and back, his arms criss-crossed about his abdomen.

Marie looked toward the boy. He was watching her. Watching the followers. Then her again. His drumbeats slowed, grew quieter, then still. The silence was loud. The followers stopped dancing, loose-limbed like rag dolls. DuLac seemed hungover.

Marie was sorry no miracle had occurred. Sorry she wasn't the one—Marie, the descendant of a Voodoo Queen.

The drummer said, *"Je regrette."* He left first, then the others, their heads and shoulders bowed with grief. Single file, the disappointed followers shuffled their way to the door.

Reneaux collapsed onto his knees. Chicken's blood overflowed the pan.

DuLac patted her back. "Tomorrow."

* * *

Connected to DuLac's guest room was a courtyard patio overflowing with tangled vines, flowers, and potted plants. Marie kept the French doors open. She wanted to feel the languid heat, see robins, pigeons bobbing their heads into the gurgling fountain, and hear the whirr of hummingbirds and bees.

Reneaux held her hand. "I've a meeting tomorrow with FBI poison specialists."

"You think the women were poisoned?"

"Not sure. But I want to get to forensics. Make sure tissue samples are left."

"That's more practical than what I'm doing."

"No. You've got to believe."

"Why?"

"Because DuLac believes in you."

"And you?"

"I believe, too. So does El."

She laughed harshly. "I'm a failure but everyone believes in me. Why?"

"Maybe because we all want miracles. A belief in the spiritual."

"We should all attend Mass."

"Maybe so. The Catholic Church was divinely inspired, I do believe that. But I remember a host of Sundays where I was taught that God, Christ, the Virgin, were white. That only a priest could absolve my sins. The same priest who likely abused the altar boys. I'd rather believe in you. Believe there's more unknown than known. Mysteries. Miracles.

"You're special, Marie. I can tell by the way you love." Reneaux lifted her in his arms, carried her, and laid her gently on the bed. "Sleep," he said. "*Fais dodo.* Dream."

She dreamed Eden was just beyond the glass doors. Reneaux was scribbling music; baby Marie was crawling in the garden, and she was on the bed, her belly round.

* * *

She woke to drums. Moonlight filtered through leaves. Marie could see fireflies, mosquitoes seesawing the air.

The door opened, a sliver of light highlighted DuLac, rendering him gigantic in the doorway.

"You didn't wake me."

"You needed the rest. 'Sides I was hoping the *loas* would wake you."

She sat; the sheet fell around her waist. She was in a white shift. The supplicants must've dressed her—washed, dried, and rubbed cocoa oil on her limbs for the ceremony. She didn't remember the women's hands, didn't remember their sweet care.

"Reneaux?"

"He's back. Waiting for you."

She stood. She heard the flourish of a drum. Though she didn't step in time to the beat, she felt it in her heart.

Legba, remove the barrier for me.
Legba, remove the barrier so I may pass through.

They walked down the hall and paused before the red door. DuLac nodded. "Eh, yé, yé, Maman Marie."

"Eh, yé, yé," the spirits in the room responded.

Marie stepped inside.

The drummer boy grinned at Marie. His fingers and palms flew over the drums. Sweat cascaded down his arms.

Petey sucked on a pipe, pounding a walking stick. His beat counterpointed the drums. An old woman sashayed her hips and coquettishly waved a fan. Another man with a blade sliced and jabbed the air. El dipped her hips and swayed. Her feet stepping delicately; her fingers shooing invisible demons.

"The spirits have been waiting," said DuLac. "That's Legba. He came first, opening the gate. That's Ezili. The Goddess of Love. Most like the Virgin. A brown-eyed beauty. And Agwé, the sea god. Madame Thornton is touched by Ogun, the warrior god. He fights his enemies without mercy."

Marie inhaled, exhaled. The drum grew louder, more intense. Sound echoed off the walls.

Reneaux was sitting cross-legged in the corner, his head bent. Kind Dog's head rested on his lap.

"Kind Dog has been to ceremonies before," said DuLac. "How else to explain his calm?"

Kind Dog tilted his head upward. Marie couldn't help feeling that he was telling her not to fear. The drumming tonight, unlike the bayou drums, didn't scare him.

She bent before Reneaux. The dancers whirled behind her. Kind Dog nuzzled her hand.

She felt a rush of goodwill toward Reneaux. He was a sweet,

loving man. She caressed his face. Reneaux looked up; he wasn't there. *Someone else was locked behind his irises.*

"*Who killed your Maman?*"

She tried to escape, but the spirit inside Reneaux held her. Gripped both her arms.

"*Who murdered her?*"

Murdered? The word burrowed into Marie's soul, unleashing raw feelings, releasing her unconscious to follow a trail, a yellow brick road of awareness and pain.

"*There were signs.*"

"No."

"Think back." DuLac squatted, whispering in her ear. "You've always been able to see."

What did she see? Truly?

"Think back."

Bits of salt tossed in the corner. Feathers on the windowsill. Markings on the stoop; her mother washing the steps with herbs and lye.

Ogun was drawing Marie into the room's center, the circle's heart. Dancers swayed around her; the drum sounded like a hundred.

"Remember, Marie," DuLac shouted.

Reneaux, as Ogun, screamed, "Murderer. Murder."

Kind Dog chased his tail.

"Remember."

She remembered: *Mother, fretful, days before her death. She'd kept the shades drawn, made the sign of the cross a hundred times a day. She drew markings of the crucifix on the wall, the door, and floors. She prayed constantly to the Virgin. Rattled her rosary beads between her thumbs.*

"Remember."

*Mother fell, her hands still wet. Water still flowing from the tap.
But there'd been a pot on the stove. An empty cup on the table.*

Something in the tea . . .

Eh, yé, yé, Maman Marie.

Eh, yé, yé, Maman Marie.

She weaves spells, she makes gris-gris.

She has the power, Maman Marie.

DuLac chanted; the followers echoed him. Staccato drumming filled the space between heartbeats, between breaths.

Marie screamed.

"Call the gods, Marie." It was DuLac. "Call the gods."

"Mother, please." She was a child again, needing her mother. "Mother. Help me, please."

She was in a whirlwind. Spirals of mist lined the ceiling. Arms upraised, she shouted, "Come."

Her mother dove inside her and, for a moment, she felt intense love. Then confusion, sorrow, more pain than a heart could stand.

"You are me," her mother murmured. And she was—feeling her mother's fear, the years, months, days, hours, and minutes of hiding from herself. Hiding from a stalker who'd discovered who and where she was, who'd taunted her for days before her death.

Reneaux held Kind Dog as if his life depended upon it. DuLac slit a chicken's throat. A balding man, a water spirit, was rowing ashore. The other loas were dancing. Legba shook his stick at Ezili. Ogun slew invisible warriors.

How silly to think that the dead could become undead. Silly

to think that love for her mother could revive, resurrect her. She was dreaming. Nothing more than vivid memories. Vivid dreams.

"Damballah is Father to all the gods," DuLac heralded:

> Damballah is a snake.
> If you see Marie Laveau, you see a snake.
> You see Damballah-wedo.

Everyone, including Reneaux, was chanting:

> Damballah-wedo. Marie Laveau is a snake.

Marie turned slightly, staring at the canvas. *Colors were moving, shifting shape again. Oil figures mirrored the dancers in the room. Legba was inside the landscape; so, too, DuLac, El, and Reneaux. Kind Dog was sitting, his back against the cathedral wall.*

Where was she?

Marie entered from offstage, a snake curled about her arm.

Marie felt the snake, slithering against flesh. She closed her eyes. It wasn't real. None of it was real.

The snake slid across her chest, its head lifting toward her neck, its body trailing the valley between her breasts, its tail draped down about her waist.

It wasn't there.

The snake touched her neck—curling, tightening about her throat. She couldn't breathe. Her life was draining out of her.

"Damballah," she screamed; for a flickering moment, she saw the snake, its yellow eyes aligned with hers.

"I believe."

She felt the snake's body uncurl, then felt its weight lift, disappear from her throat.

"Call the gods, Marie."

Mother was in the painting again, cradling the snake.

"Damballah-wedo. Marie Laveau is a snake." Followers chanted, the rhythm and volume increasing.

The woman in the painting smiled. Mother's face. Then hers. Then someone else.

Ride her? Isn't that what DuLac had said?

She felt two women, touching her heart, soul, and mind. Two women loving her down through the generations, across time and space. Of the two, her mother was weaker. It was the third Marie that made her strong.

"Give in to the ride, Marie. Give in."

She slid to the floor. Dancers encircled her.

Outside the circle, she saw Reneaux, on his hands and knees, shouting. Kind Dog barked excitedly. She saw snatches of Reneaux and Dog between the flowing skirts, the stomping feet, the click of the cane, and the sword slicing air.

DuLac was encouraging, "Go, let yourself go."

She slid like a snake, saw the Guédé, standing in the corner, tipping their hats; one clapped his gloved hands.

She exhaled and two spirits—one Mother's?—flew out of her mouth.

El began shrieking, tossing her hands into the air, spinning then slowing like a childhood top.

The drumming was thunderous.

Bright sun. Bright moon. Day became night then day then night again. Marie could feel the breeze kicked up by the dancers' skirts.

Feel the floor tremble. Smell the musk. Hear the slowing, softening of the drum.

"Mon piti bébé. Mon piti bébé." *It was Mother's voice.*

El, but not El, crawled into the room's heart, its center. The dancers, subdued, watchful, encircled her and Marie.

"Mother?"

"Don't touch her," shouted DuLac.

"I love you. Always have. Always will."

"I miss you."

Guédé, hats off, heads bowed, wailed silently, wept bitter tears.

"Dead, undead. Should've told you." Eyes closed, El's chin rested on her chest.

"Mother, stay. Please."

"Sorry," she sighed. "I wasn't dead."

El fell slowly sideways, almost as if someone were laying her down to sleep.

The drumming stopped. *"Mother!" Spirits flew.* Bodies arched and ached; followers were tired and old again.

Honeysuckle lingered in the air.

"Don't touch," shouted DuLac. "Let El recover. She'll be fine."

Marie held on to Reneaux; he stroked her hair.

The room was hushed, except for panting. Winded souls recovering.

"What did she mean? Dead, undead?"

"In voodoo, all things alive. Always there are spirits. Ancestors. Your mother crossed over, spoke to you. That's all. *Vite.* Ceremony ended."

"All things alive." Her mother's words, written in script. *"Snakes are stirring in your blood."*

166

El rubbed her eyes, like a child awakening from sleep.

Followers stepped forward, ignoring El, yet touching, bowing to Marie. One kissed her hand. Another, her skirt's hem. Still another touched his lips to the floor.

The drummer boy bowed, swept his drum over his shoulder. "We did good."

"Go home, go home." DuLac was shooing his guests. "The spirits are gone."

"Not quite," Marie told DuLac. *She felt some shift in the air, a current between this world and another. An insistent whisper: "The blood is alive. Always."*

"No more will happen tonight. When the ceremony is over, it's over." DuLac was pacing the room, as though by squaring all the corners he could somehow contain the room's experiences.

Marie grabbed his hand; she felt him trembling. Was he scared? Shaken because not once had a spirit visited him? Upset because a woman had surpassed him?

DuLac's expression was clear, without guile. Without jealousy. Envy.

"Let's get a drink."

"No. You're not telling me something."

"I've told you enough."

She released his hand; he stood, watching over her, staring down from afar.

Sitting on the floor, seeing the ceremony's debris, Marie wondered if she'd made a mistake. *Had anything really happened?* Except for DuLac, they were all sprawled on the floor like children. Candles still flickered; the painting was muted, dull. The chicken was stiffening; blood drained over the shallow tray. Trays of seeds, cornmeal, and water lay on the altar. The saints were cheap plaster; the rosary beads, plastic. As if left by messy children playing dress-up, Legba's cane was propped in the corner. Ezili's fan spread like a broken accordion on the floor. Ogun's sword stuck outside a straw basket. The Guédé were gone.

El, disoriented, leaned against Reneaux. "You should rest," Reneaux said, helping her to rise.

Marie studied her dusty hands, nails cracked from clutching and crawling across the floor. Her dress and feet were dirty, too. She'd been a snake, been touched by a spirit. She'd heard a voice she hadn't heard in eighteen years. *Smelled honeysuckle. Smelled it still. Heard a faint whispering. An answer in the beating of her own heart.* DuLac was wrong; spirits still lingered; spirits existed outside the boundaries of a ceremony.

Fiercely, she clutched DuLac's hands, pulling him down until his knees touched hers.

"Dead, undead. What does it mean?"

"It means buried alive."

She knew she was screaming but she couldn't hear herself. She was in the fun house again, the room upended, sinister.

She slipped unconscious, swallowed by a nightmare, the other spirit, the third Marie, whispered, "All will be made right."

* * *

She woke, feeling the others—El, Reneaux, DuLac—moving through the house like ghosts. She was on the couch. A blanket tucked about her.

How long had she been unconscious?

Above the fireplace was the painting of the ceremony in

Cathedral Square. Except, she now knew, this wasn't the real one—the magical canvas, the one that knew all the secrets.

Still, the woman in this painting was neither her nor her mother. It was the ancestor. The third Marie. The one who'd swept inside her with Maman.

Dead, undead.

Her teeth digging into her lip, Marie tasted blood. What would it have felt like?

In medical terms, she knew the steps. There'd be panic. Pulse, metabolic rate would race. Oxygen would be used up faster. Maybe there'd be five minutes of air in the coffin. As oxygen decreased, there'd be more carbon dioxide. The victim would hyperventilate. After ten minutes, not enough air to feed energy reactions in the body—neurons firing, the heart pumping, there'd be flailing attempts to open the coffin. Blood oxygen levels drop. Blood circulates but has nothing to feed the cells.

So, cells die.

First, brain cells. The victim would fall unconscious. Only autonomic responses active—the body still trying to breathe, pump blood. More brain cells lost. Brain death. Autonomic responses begin to fail. The heart stops pumping, the lungs stop struggling for air.

Death.

She couldn't imagine the horror, the pain. Ten minutes that would seem like ten hours, fighting for one's life.

All this time, she'd been focused on loss—losing a mother, not having a father or family. Fighting the loneliness of living in a stranger's home. Her foster mother, Mrs. Harris, taking a belt to her back and arms for the pleasure of it. Her husband, elderly and impotent, slyly caressing her breasts and buttocks. As she grew, she learned to lock doors, escape the house, dress in over-sized clothes. None of her trials compared with her mother's.

Dead, undead.

She'd heard Mother's voice floating out of El's body.

It happened. It was real. She was a doctor. She'd seen miracles, amazing recoveries: a man overcoming the paralysis of a stroke; a blue baby beginning to breathe; a woman, infertile, delivering a child; a cancer patient outrunning death's odds; and a baby alive inside a dead mother's womb.

Dead, undead.

Doctor Mary, Marie Levant. A scientist. Rational. "Don't get emotional," Dr. Levant. Dr. Levant who dreamed about the past and the future, experienced visions, spoke with spirits, smelled, felt, and saw things unseen.

All things alive.

Poor Maman. Murdered. Dead, undead.

So there were two types of death, undeath—buried in a casket, deep underground; the second, a resurrected spirit still haunted by how she died.

The blood is alive.

Blood connecting her to her mother, Marie-Claire, and the baby. All the Maries. But it was ancestor Marie who'd swept inside her, who was strongest. Tough. It was this Marie who healed. This Marie who'd help her avenge her mother's murder.

Kind Dog's nose brushed her hand. She rubbed his head. The brown-eyed dog blinked. "Let's solve mysteries."

She stood. The floor held steady. One step, two. Kind Dog, as if trained to heel, kept in step beside her.

Voices, sibilant and murmuring, came from the kitchen. She looked back at the painting. All still. No shapes shifting. The woman was banana-colored. Thick brows, full lips. High cheekbones, perhaps from a native descendant (hadn't some Louisianans mixed with Choctaws?). She had long, black hair; her body was rounded, curved. Her arms were open, inviting the supplicants, the frenzied dancers close. This was the "Queen" her mother had told tales about.

Marie crossed the hall. It was all new territory. Like a blind woman, she felt the wall. Kind Dog's body brushed against her calves.

Someone else brushed past them both, calling her name, "Marie Levant. Marie Levant. Marie Levant née Marie Laveau."

Marie Levant born Marie Laveau.

* * *

"The women . . . the young girls weren't dead."

Reneaux set down his whiskey glass; DuLac stopped stirring gumbo; El laid a deuce on her solitaire deck.

"Not possible," El said.

"Everything's possible," said DuLac.

"But that child, Marie-Claire, was dead. Marie operated on her. Sliced through her abdomen and womb. All those girls were dead."

Kind Dog sat. Marie looked at a weary DuLac. Reneaux pulled out his spiral pad. El stared at her cards as if she could prophesy.

"How do you know this, Marie?"

"I just know, Reneaux."

"Here." DuLac handed her a whiskey shot.

171

"Medically it's impossible. I checked the women myself. I was there when my mother died. Except she wasn't dead." She clamped her mouth shut, swallowing bile. She remembered her knife slicing through skin.

"It could happen," said DuLac. "I've never seen it. But old *houngans* telling about older *houngans*. Mainly in Haiti. Priestesses telling of perversions from the nineteenth, eighteenth centuries. They tell about deep trances. Trances where a soul loses its will."

"Mind control?" asked Reneaux.

"Maybe. Maybe something else. I don't know. I do know there are piles of dissertations in university libraries about folks, with no medical cause, believing they're going to die, then dying. They call it voodoo but it's not. Just plain evil. Hexes, voodoo dolls. Evil business. Such charms don't have power, except in weak people's minds."

"Just great. Tell my Chief that evil is killing young girls."

"'Tis true. Plenty sin in New Orleans."

"Sin comes from evil," caroled El.

"Everybody in New Orleans believes in voodoo—most believe it's evil, like the Hollywood garbage of 'goats without horns,' black folks sacrificing white babies. Or like the erotic, racist view of white masters believing slaves had loose morals, and voodoo was 'night dancing,' a prelude to sex. Only a few, like those who came tonight, believe in the real voodoo, the helping and the healing. White culture has denigrated African-based faiths until most modern folks want nothing to do with them. Tell your Chief it's voodoo and he'll quake in his shoes. But voodoo isn't evil. Not the faith. People sin."

Reneaux chewed on his pen. "You sure, Marie?"

"I'm sure."

"Controlled? So thoroughly you'd allow yourself to be placed in a grave?"

"Zombies," said El.

"*Non*," said DuLac. "Only one *zombi*—Damballah, *li Grand Zombi*. He has the power of faith, possession. Damballah's not evil."

"So the movies are wrong," drawled Reneaux, sarcastic. "Undead still sounds like zombies to me."

DuLac shifted awkwardly. He slowly stirred okra, crayfish, simmering on the stove. "Not just from Haiti. From Laveau's day. Laveau's husband. She tells how he felt nothing."

"If zombies are real, then I believe in vampires," said El, sarcastic.

"Whoever heard of a black vampire?"

"Blade," said El. "That Wesley Snipes man."

"Naw," Reneaux drawled, "don't count. Blade's half human."

El laughed, high-pitched. DuLac shook his head. Reneaux chuckled, slapping his notebook on his thigh.

"Stop it. All of you. Just shut up." Marie was furious. Dog growled. He stood in front of Marie, the hair on his spine upraised, his bandaged leg leaning awkwardly.

Reneaux stood, quickly patting the dog. "Settle down, Dog." He gathered Marie in his arms. "We're sorry. No harm," he said. "No harm. Just some humor. Otherwise we'd all go crazy." He kissed her brow.

"Consult an ancient book for an ancient evil."

"What do you mean, DuLac?"

He shook his head. "Eat first. Else you won't make it 'til morn." He ladled stew.

"I'll make coffee," said El.

Reneaux encouraged Marie and Kind Dog to sit.

Way past midnight, the sky, a soft black, fireflies blinking in the night air, the four of them ate at the kitchen table. Drinking coffee with chicory and milk, spicing their gumbo with hot sauce, they worried in companionable silence. Kind Dog snored. His bandaged paw batted the air like he was dreaming.

* * *

"I've heard tell of a fish. Mentioned in a journal I have."

"So it's a drug," said Reneaux.

"*Non,* evil, I told you," snapped DuLac.

"Drugs can be evil."

Marie heard Reneaux's fury edged with bitterness.

He flipped open his notepad. "Doesn't make sense. Women pregnant, made to appear dead. Why? Standard tests have been done. No known detectable poison. No known detectable anything. Except awash in pregnancy hormones. Like they'd been given huge doses. Not just pregnant. But very pregnant."

"Why didn't you tell us?" asked Marie.

"You think it's significant?"

"Might be."

"How much of this is science fiction or science fact?" queried El.

"What do you think, Marie?" asked DuLac.

"The scientist in me says, 'No'; this other part of me says, 'Yes.'"

"Any tissue samples left?"

"The FBI has them. They've contacted Caribbean and African specialists in folk medicine."

"Good, Reneaux."

"And what about the mark?" asked Marie. "The upside-down cross with a snake, sloped like a sideways S?"

"Means nothing as far as I can tell," said Reneaux. "I've searched for the symbol everywhere. Santeria, Haitian *Voudon*, Candomblé, Rastafarian movements, even Catholic theology. The only connection I've found is to supposed Satanic groups, European-based, with the snake representing the Devil."

"Religions from the African Diaspora all value the snake as knowledge, all-knowing, an infinity and fertility symbol. White Christians bemoan that a snake tempted Eve in the Garden. But in voodoo, the same myth is a cause for celebration. Snakes represent knowledge. 'Knowing' is what keeps you safe, strong. What good is Eden with ignorance?"

"Maybe its a red herring," said Reneaux, "something to throw us off the scent?"

"From Mister Evil?"

"You think it's a man, DuLac?" asked Marie.

"I do."

"Why not either? Or both? A woman and a man."

"Marie, you're thinking of the DeLaCroixs," said Reneaux. "I've already been out to see them. Twice. Trail's dead."

"Still, the baby's grandmother didn't seem innocent. The mother sounded as if she was cruel."

El patted Marie's knee. "The baby's fine."

Marie's chair screeched. Kind Dog scooted up awkwardly.

"You don't understand. It's not about the baby."

None of them looked at her. Reneaux scribbled with his pencil; DuLac dipped another bread piece in the stew; and El hummed a tune in the back of her throat.

"I want to go home."

"I'll drive you." Reneaux opened the screen door. Pink and a burnt orange were far off in the horizon.

Marie abruptly turned back. "You've known me."

"Since you were a babe," said DuLac.

"Who am I?"

"Isn't it clear? Laveau's descendent, a link in a long line of Voodoo Queens."

"That's what frightened my mother?"

"The corruption, the bastardization. Hard for voodoo to survive in the New World. She didn't take time to understand the real voodoo. She didn't feel the healing we felt tonight."

"Healing? I didn't help anyone."

"Yourself." DuLac gently cupped her face. "Since you were a child, you've been preparing. To be a healer. That's what voodoo is—healing bodies, souls, and minds."

"Then why am I ill?" she said harshly. "Sickened by everything I've seen and heard tonight?"

"You'll thrive when you understand who you be. Wait." He opened a side pantry door.

El tapped her nails on the table. "I'm not sure about zombies, but you've got to believe in what happened tonight. Reneaux, don't say a word. You felt it, too."

Reneaux closed his mouth.

"Do you believe, El?"

"Of course she believes," said DuLac, shouting from the

pantry, one side filled with shelves of canned goods, flour, and rice; the other side filled with oils, herbs, and roots, labeled in bottles. He reached for a book on the highest shelf. "Good and evil always battling. Whether folks be Catholic, Protestant, voodoo, don't matter. Faith wins the fight. Do you believe, Marie? In what happened tonight? In you?"

DuLac stood tall and strong before her. He held the book as an offering.

Marie searched her heart. "Yes," she said simply. "Yes."

"*Bon.* This is for you."

Journal of Louis DeLavier, 18—.

Marie gently clutched the book, feeling emotions welling through leather, paper, and ink.

"DeLavier loved Marie Laveau. He captured her story when she was dying. 'Cept Marie Laveau didn't die, she was waiting. For you—"

Marie caressed the spine, the fragile pages.

"—a strong woman with a pure heart. Queen. Queen Laveau. Queen of the Old and the New. Voodoo Queen."

THE END

Two Thousand and Five

The most feared evil in voodoo is a zombie. Resurrected, mind-less, soulless bodies are controlled by a priest, an evil houngan. Souls from resurrected bodies roam the earth in torment.

To prevent zombies, "Make sure your loved ones are indeed dead and their bodies do not go warm to the grave."

—The Origins and History of the Voodoo Cults
(From Louis DeLavier's journal)

eneaux had taken her home. She wanted to be alone.
In her apartment with Kind Dog.

Her rooms had been searched and she felt violated.
The sheets were scattered. Dresser drawers upturned. Underwear
littered like small clues. Her medical jackets were ripped, piled
on the closet floor. Advil floated in the toilet. A Tampax box had
been shredded as if it might've held secret treasure, a miniature
map. The kitchen smelled of ketchup and soured milk. Marie
stepped gingerly over broken glass. The freezer door had been
left open. Strawberry ice cream dripped on the floor. Foil pack-
ages of chicken were soft. She imagined rot inside the glittering
wrap.

Reneaux righted a lamp, picked a pillow off the floor.

"Leave it."

"You shouldn't be here, Marie."

"He won't come back." She knew it was true.

"I don't like this."

She kissed Reneaux, knowing he wanted to stay. But she needed to read the journal alone. Think on her mother's death, alone. Quell her fears.

"Lock the door."

"I will. I promise." One, two, three locks. Marie knew spirits could easily walk through wood. They'd entered her flesh, her soul; they'd entered her dreams. But she wanted to pretend privacy was possible.

Her medical bag had been emptied, kicked aside. Marie picked it up, grateful she'd had the foresight to add a false lining. She pulled out the velvet pouch, emptied the rosary, the Virgin images onto the bed. Her mother's handwriting comforted her.

The scotch was half full. She took a swig from the bottle, laid the journal on the mattress beside Kind Dog. She swallowed another shot.

She could see Jacques, his long legs extending past the edge of the bed. He smiled at her, even patted Dog. "Chérie," she heard him call. "Chérie." Then he disappeared.

She opened the journal. *The pages shimmered alive:*

"A story should begin at the beginning. But in this story, the middle is the beginning. Everything spirals outward from the center. Lies, pain, and loss haunt the future as well as the past.

"Grandmére, my mother, my daughter, myself—we were all named Marie. This story is all of us. Be sure to write everything down, Louis.

"Voodoo is worth passing on." Marie Laveau—1881.

Marie could almost see Laveau, old and dying, telling her story, passing it down through the generations, passing it to her.

From dawn to dusk, Marie read DeLavier's journal. It was two

*hn who'd called: "See here. Witness a miracle. Marie
es zombies." While the crowd roared approval.*

opped reading. She couldn't catch her breath. Kind

*t as if some spirit was pushing her, trying to delve
e fell back upon the bed. Rainbow colors floated on the
l Dog was snuffling her, whimpering, pushing against
d arm.*

*l feel herself leaving, disappearing from the concrete
outlines of the room dissolving, the bed becoming
Even Kind Dog was fading, his smell and sounds dis-*

*ack in time. Almost as if she was inside DuLac's paint-
he ceremony was on a lakeshore. There were thousands,
ls—black, white, free and enslaved followers dressed in
s dressed in outrageous purple, red, and black, wearing
ardi Gras masks.*

*Laveau, young and heart-stricken, screaming to wake
cques stood dull-eyed, center stage, in a filthy sailor's
is clothes hung loosely, as if, soulless, his body had
ze. His skin lacked color and his hair was matted and
arms dangled. To the crowd, Jacques was the bogey-
o life. He was the ghost who'd haunted their childhood
ere was nothing in the world more horrible than*

*urned, appealing to Marie. Seeing her ancestor, rem-
family history, an echo of her features, there was no
e the call.
dead.*

confessions. DeLavier's confession of love for Marie. How he adored her! Marie's confession of how as a woman, as a priestess sometimes her power and will hadn't been enough. She'd been the most feared woman in New Orleans and she'd been the most human. Frail, in her own way, and searching.

The yellowed pages were filled with complications. Marie understood white against black, rich against poor, men against women, good against evil. In the twenty-first century, discrimination hadn't disappeared. She didn't understand faith and miracles. Women walking on air. Sinners given salvation. A snake representing knowledge as good. Or Catholicism and voodoo blending as naturally as tea leaves with water. Mysteries abounded.

"Women hand sight down through the generations. Mother to daughter."

Except in Laveau's life, the line had been broken. Laveau's grandmother (just like Marie's mother) had hidden the faith. Misguided love had made the children vulnerable.

But now Marie understood that coming to New Orleans had been her *fa,* her fate. *"Can't escape* fa," the journal said.

On and on she read:

She and Laveau were both orphans. She remembered the dream: *a woman grown, strapped to a tree, scars crisscrossing her back.* That had been Laveau's mother—captured by whites, murdered during a ceremony. *She remembered an old woman singing, "Guédé, Guédé, have mercy."* That was Laveau's Grandmère; but it was also the Madame DeLaCroix at Breezy's. Baby Marie's grandmother.

Marie's heart raced.

She, trembling, diving into thick, heady water, catfish brushing her thighs. That had to be Marie Laveau, her moment of triumph when she walked across Lake Pontchartrain, as if it were earth. Nonsense. Impossible. But the miracle was recorded in the journal, and in a newspaper clipping tucked in the journal's pages.

What was the last part of her dreaming?

She, a mother, screaming, giving birth, as she, the babe, slipped out, swimming downstream in a rush of water, a bloodied, blue-red membrane covering her face.

Baby Marie had been born with a caul. She wasn't the mother but she felt as though she was. If it hadn't been for her, the baby would've died.

Kind Dog nuzzled her, curled up, warm, against her abdomen.

She lay back against the pillow. In her dream, she'd been everyone. The links—the generations collapsed across time. She sat up quickly, skipping ahead to the journal's last chapter. Two hours before she died, Laveau repeated to DeLavier:

"Life is a spiral. The only protection is to become disembodied—to see the self as other. Immortal.

"The generations are overlapping. Women hand sight down through the generations.

"One generation will get it right."

Was that her calling? To get it right?

Even Marie Laveau couldn't save her loved ones. Her life had been filled with betrayal.

John, her nemesis, had manipulated her gifts to gain money and power. Killed her Grandmère.

As someone had killed her mother. Marie took another shot from the bottle.

She was at a crossroads. Frighte
What would her mother have
she hid, her life would be lonely a
She didn't understand much
*voodoo taught that all things—an
things were signs.*
She realized she'd been trying
tory repeats," the journal said.
Unless she could get it right. Resl
Laveau had been a child, only
Marie was a woman grown. A do
DuLac. And she had Laveau, h
journal to chart a path.
But she hadn't finished the sto
"Consult an ancient book for an
She read on. Dusk gave way
ten, eleven.
Laveau's husband was nam
coincidence.

Zombie. Zombie.
Marie Laveau makes
Walking dead. The u
Marie Laveau makes

Except that was a lie. There
The snake god. Just as DuLac
python. Zombie was an aberra
From those who aligned voodo

*It w
Laveau
Mar
Dog he
Mar
inside
ceiling.
She
world.
epheme
solving.
She
ing, exce
not hur
white. C
grotesqu
She s
the dead
uniform.
shrunk i
tangled.
man com
dreams.
Jacques.
Laveau
nants of
way to ig
Dead,*

A hundred and fifty years later. She was chosen to finish the battle.

* * *

Marie gulped air—like a negative developing, her surroundings became concrete, color filled in the shapes. She was here. In this reality.

She could feel her flesh tingling, hear her heart's murmur. Smell Kind Dog's fur. See him watching her, his nose moist, his brows arched, curious. She patted his head. "You are one pretty dog." Black hair, brown-eyed. Compassionate.

* * *

Marie went to her balcony. It was dawn again. The city had always been two cities: the past and the present. The culture had been infused with slaves, immigrants, soldiers, opportunists. Great good had happened. Great evil, too. She blinked. *Like a veil lifting, she could see the human drama Laveau had been a part of—slave auctions, street vendors, elegant French ladies shopping with black footmen carrying their parasols and hatboxes, priests decrying licentiousness, and drunken sailors being seduced and rolled by prostitutes. Sidewalks were made of wood, streets littered with horse manure; carriage tracks etched in mud like a mad maze.* She blinked again: Hawkers were heralding escort services, X-rated shows, corner stands sold juleps, taffy, and brittle candy, tourists shopped for T-shirts, an evangelist propped on a box warned of the apocalypse and seamen heckled transvestites and slovenly drunks.

This was her city—her home.

Here, she'd find herself. Here, she'd find who killed her mother. Here, she'd find who was murdering young girls. She had a purpose now. Not a bad way to live or die. Like the ER, she was beating back the odds, beating back the Devil.

The phone rang. Kind Dog barked at the receiver.

She picked up the phone, knowing it was Reneaux, knowing what he was going to say before he said it.

"Another girl dead."

He hung up; she listened to the static on the wire.

* * *

Pride.

She'd been focusing on marshaling her strength and another daughter, a child had been dying. Marie collapsed into a chair, her face in her hands. What good were visions if they were after the fact?

Who did she think she was?

An orphan. Foster child. Not even a licensed doctor. A woman—like the victims.

She shuddered. Kind Dog rubbed his back against her legs. She bent, cradling him, her head resting atop his spine.

"*Je suis Marie.*" She lifted her head. "*Je suis Marie.*" It was Laveau's voice. *I am Marie.* A simple declaration. But more than that. Laveau spoke the words to affirm she was strong. She said it when John tried to manipulate her. She said it when she'd lost track of her soul, her self. When she felt vulnerable beyond measure. *Je suis. I am.*

Marie Levant, not perfect. She was who she was. I am.

Marie heard a trumpet blare. Loud enough to bring down Jericho's walls. To call Gabriel to Kingdom Come. Three long, wailing blasts. Defiant. Outraged. The sound became a keening wail. Then the notes swirled into the melody: "Go Down, Body. Lay My Body Down."

Marie went to the balcony, gripping the railing. Over rooftops she could see St. Louis Cathedral. See mourners coming out of the church and a black and antique gold carriage with stallions (feathers sticking skyward from their manes) pulling a coffin on a flatbed hearse. Kind Dog barked wildly. She looked down. *The snakes on the rail were moving, slithering end to end. Iron was as malleable as clay.*

She saw the nineteenth-century world blending with the twenty-first, the spirit with the real. Parallel worlds merging. There was substance in the air. An intangible feeling that grief was necessary for instruction.

She dashed into her apartment. Some instinct made her remove the rosary from the pouch.

"Stay, Dog." He howled.

But she needed to move fast, race down the stairs, faster than the elevator, dash across streets, through cobblestone alleys to Cathedral Square. Mist covered the Gulf; oil pools made rainbows on the road.

Two other trumpets joined the fiercely melancholic one. A clarinet added a whine and a snare drum rolled a steady, funeral beat. Five brilliant-black musicians. A concert master waved his hands like batons and the rhythm shifted from a drone to a celebration. "Oh, when the saints . . . oh, when the saints go marchin' in . . ."

> I am just a lonesome traveler,
> Through this big wide world of sin;
> Want to join that grand procession,
> When the saints go marchin' in.

191

Oh, when the saint go marchin' in,
Lord, I want to be in that number
When the saints go marchin' in.

Marie saw the Guédé clapping, their white gloves fluttering like doves' wings. In unison, they tipped their hats. She nodded. *And they clapped again, this time for her. Two danced a spontaneous minuet, bowing and weaving, stepping primly forward and back.*

Women with parasols were twirling, skipping behind the hearse as it stately turned out of the square toward Riverwalk and St. Louis Cemetery.

There was a man dressed like a Guédé—in top hat and tuxedo tails, his gloved hands offering engraved cards.

"*Mademoiselle.*"

She flipped over the card: "To everything there is a season." Ecclesiastes 3:1–8.

Marie studied the sharp-faced man. "Who died?"

"One of the Pietre twins. Ninety, if she's a day. Other one gonna go soon. Old maids. Never married. *C'est vrai.* That's why all the folks come. Really two funerals, not one. Good time, good day to die. Guédé happy; mourners happy."

"You see the Guédé?"

"*Oui.* They over there." He pointed at a lamppost. Marie realized he didn't see any spirits at all. *The Guédé were frolicking, crawling all over the hearse.*

Marie handed him back his card. The Guédé man sniffed and walked away.

Unlike for her mother, Marie appreciated that the Pietre mourners were many. Dozens of family and friends, even strangers who'd been partying all night, and early morning Mass celebrants who respected an unknown woman's passing. A perfect time for a funeral, just past dawn before the streets were crowded and the sun too high.

The surviving sister, tiny, no more than five feet, draped in black satin and veil, was escorted by two middle-aged women. Marie felt the old woman staring at her. Her head tilted like a bird's.

In a reedy voice, the Pietre twin squealed, "I know you. I know you," and moved toward Marie with a surprising spryness and grace.

"Auntie. You don't know this woman."

A priest was watching from the steps.

"I do." The woman lifted her veil; to Marie, it was clear it didn't matter. The woman's eyes were blue marbles, cataract-blind.

"I apologize," said the elder escort.

"No need," said Marie.

The Pietre twin clutched Marie's fingertips. "My sister and I know Madame Laveau. Every goodbye ain't gone. Every goodbye ain't gone."

"What do you mean?"

"She visits us every Mardi Gras. I always leave out a bit of wild rice. Lemonade, too."

"Excuse her. Our aunt is old-school. Believing in superstitious, voodoo stuff."

"You, nothing but silly new school. No more sense than a cricket." The small, elflike twin batted her niece's hands away. She crooked her finger at Marie. Marie bent, her ear turned toward the old woman's mouth.

"She told us you were coming. Said I'd live to see it. I'm Bettina. My sister was Luanne. Sister be so happy when I tell her tonight. Everybody thinks she's gone but she ain't. Just like Madame Laveau. She—we—been waiting a long time for you."

Bettina had the sweetest smile. Marie hugged and kissed the small woman. Her skin felt like soft crepe.

The two nieces, annoyed, steered Bettina away.

"Say prayers," the old woman shouted, gleeful.

"I will."

Bettina stepped lightly, shaking her shoulders to the marching beat. Not at all sad to be attending her sister's funeral.

Marie couldn't help smiling. She felt she was herself yet not herself—a collection of ancestors. Bettina was right. The dead weren't gone.

The black-robed priest, as white as the moon, watched her. Then he turned and went inside the church. Marie felt compelled to follow him. She stopped on the steps, watching the departing funeral, appreciating the uplifting wail of the band.

The Guédé were fluttering about Bettina, solicitous. One Guédé pulled the hat off a niece's head. The woman gasped. Bettina cackled and clapped her hands.

The human Guédé was right. Bettina was going to die soon.

* * *

The priest had disappeared. In the vestibule, red votive candles flickered and two ornate angel statues cupped their hands to hold the holy water.

She hadn't been in church for nearly two decades, not since her mother died. She dipped her fingers in the holy water, genuflected, and walked down the center aisle. The church was tomblike cool.

On the wall, the Stations of the Cross showed Christ's passion. The Twelfth Station, etched in oil, showed Jesus nailed to the cross between two criminals; mourning beneath him were John, his beloved disciple, Mary, the Virgin Mother, and Mary Magdalene, the redeemed whore.

Marie plucked the rosary from her pocket, feeling the beads.

How to reconcile two faiths? Two worlds?

She stared at the portrait. Christ in agony. Two women at his feet. *Twins.*

Faces turned, both Marys looked at her with a beatific smile.

"Can I help you?"

Startled, Marie leaped back, stuffing the rosary in her jeans pocket. "I don't think so."

She was barely literate as both a Catholic and a *voodooienne*. She wanted to confess—but how dare she? Whatever would she say? For all she knew, this priest would condemn her to the Devil.

"I've got to go."

"Wait. Your spirit needs healing."

Up close, his skin was luminescent.

"New Orleans is a city of contrasts. Ugliness. Great beauty, too. Sin and charity."

She watched him. Feeling some measure of strength in him. Commitment.

"In the summer, heat and yellow fever would consume the city. It was like opening a floodgate to the Angel of Death and the worst in human nature, too. Lime was tossed on thousands of bodies; everyone wore black armbands—for everyone knew someone who'd died; criminals and recent orphans robbed graves.

"Mosquitoes brought the fever; some said it was a strain from Africa brought with the slaves. Many believe the infection served as punishment for slavery. Marie Laveau worked beside priests. Nuns, too. Unafraid. Never once infected. Never once feverish. She could lift folks' fevers right into her hand.

"But you knew that, didn't you?"

"Why are you telling me this?"

"I'm like the mariner, I fit the story to the soul. Part of my gift. Sometimes I don't even realize I'm doing it."

Marie lowered her eyes, staring at the cracks, the centuries-old floor. *With her peripheral vision, she could see high-top button shoes from another age; leather half-boots with bits of mud and dung; and some bare feet. The priest beneath his flowing robes wore tennis shoes. Two worlds. Two realities.*

"Did all the priests welcome Laveau?"

"Some didn't. If I'd lived then, I surely would have."

"And Christ?"

"Christ, too. If he has love enough for two Marys, he has love enough for two faiths."

"It isn't at all the same."

"Isn't it? Isn't it love to embrace seeming contradictions?"

"Seeming?"

"The older I get, the more I see symmetry. Reconciling of contrasts. Opposites. Everything has its season."

His palm rested on her shoulder. His expression was solemn, but he had deep smile lines etched about his eyes.

Why did she feel she was being blessed?

She reached into her pocket. "Hold this for me, Father. Keep it safe."

"A lovely rosary. Unique. I've heard early voodoo worshipers made these rosaries with Christ and the snake god."

"Do you know why?"

"Forbidden on pain of death to practice their faith, they merged the religions. Seeing parallels. Symmetry. They could pray, hold the cross in their hand—both Christ and Damballah—and no one would ever know their secret. Wherever did you get this?"

"It belonged to my mother."

"Why give it to me? This is rare, precious."

She sighed and felt a calm wash over her. Why give it to him?

"To make sure you come back," whispered Laveau.

She turned, walking slowly at first, then faster and faster.

"Comment t'appelles-tu?" the priest called.

She smiled. *"Je suis Marie."*

"Bon. The Marys' namesake."

"Oui. I am the namesake."

Outside, she paused on the steps. No trace—neither sight nor sound—of the funeral. Inhale, exhale. The river stank. Fishermen were gutting fish, laying ice on their catch. The city was rousing for a new day. Vans delivered onions and okra for gumbo. Sanitation men sprayed the streets, clearing away last night's debris and vomit. Joggers were enjoying their morning constitutional before the air became too thick with heat and humidity. Mosquitoes carried West Nile.

Summer. Sin season. Fever season. Anything could happen. Even the undead.

She ran, feeling her heart expanding, growing big. She needed to hail a cab. Get to the hospital. It wasn't the sin of pride. She needed to believe in herself. And there was only one path to follow if she was going to save women's lives.

Madonna; Magdalene. Virgins and whores. Nothing new.

Baby makes three. A trinity. Both Marys, all of the Maries capable of motherhood, a mother's love. Capable of sisterhood. The key was to love with charity.

The priest's last words rang in her ears, "Your namesake Marie Laveau cared especially for the whores." His words had stopped her. He had a huge, incongruous smile.

"From the root word *ka*—two contrasting derivatives. *Ka*, in Germanic tradition became prostitute; in Latin, *kros* became cherish, charity. The highest form of Christian love.

See," the priest, palms open, spread wide his arms. "Faith is embracing seeming opposites."

Whether I wanted it or not, asked for it or not, people needed to believe in me.

Just as I needed to believe in myself.

—Marie Laveau, on accepting her fate as a Voodoo Queen

"Where is she? Morgue?"

"Too dangerous."

"Intensive care?"

El leaned close. "Upstairs on the surgical floor," she whispered.

Marie quickly hugged her, then slammed open the stairwell door, racing up the stairs. It was faster; more important, no one would see where she went. No clues to where the dead girl lay.

One step, two steps, two steps at a time, she raced, feeling overwhelming love for an unknown girl. Her footsteps echoed on concrete.

Chest heaving, loose tendrils from her ponytail, she stopped at the fifth floor. Quickly and quietly, she slipped past the door. Nurses moved efficiently. Gurneys rolled in and out of OR; some to be cut, others to recover from surgical wounding. The floor smelled of latex and antiseptic. Respirators, cardiac monitors, intercoms whirred, clicked, and buzzed.

She looked down the long hallway. To the left, third from the last door. *The girl was there.*

Marie wished she'd worn her medical coat. In jeans and a T-shirt, she looked like a relative. Except visiting wasn't allowed on this floor. She walked slowly, confident. *They won't see me. Won't care.* She walked past the care station: Nurses were reading, writing in charts, technicians labeled test tubes, a doctor was on the phone, reserving a table for two at eight.

At a dull green door, Marie looked right, left, then slipped inside.

Reneaux was standing watch. He didn't turn around. "What kept you?"

"Church."

Reneaux nodded. Only in New Orleans would it be credible to be possessed, then attend Mass. Sun streamed through the blinds. Reneaux's cross earring glinted.

"The station is sending over a guard."

"Your Chief believed you?"

"Not much. Only that there's a killer on the loose."

Marie leaned over the bedrail. Chestnut hair fanned over the pillow. The girl's skin was cool. Marie lifted her hand. There was no pulse, no discernible movement of her ribcage. She was pale like the moon.

"Dead?"

"I don't know." Marie lifted her eyelids. No dilation. She tapped her elbow, her kneecaps. No reflex. No expulsion of air. Or quiver of lungs.

"DuLac was given hell for bringing her here."

"Where is he?"

"Fighting with the morgue. And Severs."

"Severs?"

"One of the surgeons strenuously complained," Reneaux drawled. "DuLac punched him out."

"Good for him." She looked at the lovely girl. "Maybe not good for her."

"Guards are coming—"

"I know. You're doing everything you can, Reneaux."

He stretched his hand over the body; Marie clasped it.

"You think you can help?"

"I hope so." She dropped Reneaux's hand and lowered the top sheet. In the simple white cotton gown, the girl looked like an initiate. Her forehead had traces of dust.

Reneaux flipped open his notepad. "No name, no clue to her identity. Just like the others. This makes four. Dressed in a ball gown. Even feathers in her hair."

"Found?"

"Near the wharf. Two men trying to ditch the body. A steamboat was passing. Coast Guard saw a small boat too close. Almost in the ship's path. They hailed the craft and the men dove overboard. She was left floating in the boat."

"Her body would've been mutilated. Churned in the steamship's rollers."

"That's right. Makes me think we weren't supposed to find any of the girls. Someone's been helping us from the inside."

"Who?"

"I don't know. But I plan to find out. It also means we have no way of knowing how many. It could be eight, ten, twenty girls killed. Murdered."

"All of them somebody's child." Marie stroked the girl's forehead, then placed her palms on her abdomen. It was flat and smooth.

Her hands felt a quivering. "She's pregnant. Still early." *The Guédé appeared in the corner like watchful mimes.*

"What're you looking at?"

"You don't see them?"

"No."

She realized she accepted the Guédé, the fiercely melancholic gentlemen. She felt their outrage that someone was intruding on their territory. Interfering with death.

Reneaux was studying her.

"When's the guard coming?"

"Soon. I'll stay here 'til he comes."

Marie trembled. She stroked the girl's fingertips. Delicate like a baby's. Her breath quickened. "Don't get emotional." Solve the mystery.

Why this girl, not some other? Why the fancy gowns? Dead, undead? And she was, too, though Marie didn't know how she knew. The real crux was how to save her.

"You can do this," said Reneaux.

"You think so?

"Sure."

"You'll be beside me?"

"Always, if you want."

Marie didn't answer. And Reneaux didn't press; it was one of the things she liked about him. Neither of them moved, both focused on the girl.

The Guédé peered through the rails at the edge of the bed. There was a soft buzz from the fluorescent lights.

"Light-skinned," murmured Marie, touching the unblemished skin. "All the others were, too."

Reneaux flipped open his notepad. "You're right. In the old days, folks would've said mulattoes or quadroons."

"Meaning?"

"Mixed race. Mulatto, half-black; quadroon girls, one-quarter black, used to be mistresses for French aristocrats. Even had octoroons—one-eighth black. Another kind of slavery. Ironically, the lighter the better."

"In the journal, there was Marianne, a quadroon. 'So light she could pass for white.'"

"Like Severs."

"Yes. But Marianne was raped repeatedly. Prison guards thought her color—or lack of it—made her a special prize. They did to her what they didn't dare to do to a white woman."

"White women were for procreation. Women of color were prized for their so-called baseness, bestial instincts, their inherent promiscuous nature. As if all Africans were nothing more than rutting animals.

"But the *aristos* invented the craziest contradiction—wanting mistresses that looked like their wives, but with just enough color to make them feel uninhibited. To make them believe a young girl would welcome, even take pleasure in their advances. Another crazy thing—many of the mulatto and quadroon women thought they were superior to darker women."

"They all could be raped."

"Every mulatto or quadroon has in their family tree a darker mother who was raped. Sometimes the masters freed their light-skinned children, some passed. But here in New Orleans a whole

205

society grew, free coloreds intermarrying to keep their skin light."

"One drop of black blood," mused Marie.

"Cain's mark," said Reneaux. "Still cursed. A whole race made black because of sin. A Christian invention."

"An excuse to own slaves."

The Guédé, sorrowful, placed their top hats over their hearts and bowed their heads.

"Old Testament."

"What?"

"New Testament changed everything. Wasn't supposed to matter if you were a criminal or whore. Christian charity." In her mind's eyes, she could see the priest's face. Like clamping and tying off a wound, she felt herself healing, not hurting.

"Where's her gown, Reneaux?"

"In the closet."

Marie touched the silk gown. It was wet and bedraggled; a nurse had laid a towel on the closet floor. The dress had a low, sagging bodice, lace tucked in the corners. Peach flounces edged the hem and there was enough material to billow over a hoop slip. It was certainly old-fashioned. A gown fit for a debutante. Straight from a corrupt nineteenth century.

"Quadroon Balls," she murmured.

"There haven't been balls for over a hundred and fifty years."

"But what if someone was updating it? Selling girls to the highest bidder?"

"Prostitution with a twist." An ambulance siren whined. "The only person who can confirm your hunch is her. And she's apparently dead."

"Then why murder her again? In the Mississippi? Fodder for a steamship."

"There are simpler ways to make a girl disappear."

"Not unless appearances are deceiving." Marie punched the emergency button. Code Alert.

A nurse rushed through the door, then hesitated. Another nurse pushing a cardiac cart abruptly stopped.

"Who are you? This patient isn't supposed to be here."

"Here or not, she needs help."

"You're not authorized."

"I'm Doctor Levant. Off rotation. But a resident here."

"I don't care who you are. You're not authorized. This is the surgical ward."

"I am." Reneaux flicked open his badge. "Authorized."

"As am I," said DuLac, coming up from behind the two nurses. One, sturdy and authoritative; the other, young and wide-eyed, interested in the gossip she'd have to tell.

"DuLac, I didn't know this was your patient."

"Tell her what you need, Marie."

"Full Code."

The lead nurse lifted the patient's wrist. "She's dead."

DuLac smiled ruefully. "Is she, Marie?"

"No," she said, emphatic. "She's not. It's a Code."

The lead nurse hesitated.

"Just do it," said Marie. "Or I'll have you up before the board. It's a Code. I need a respirator. Fetal monitor, too."

"This patient isn't scheduled for surgery. She shouldn't be here."

"Do it," said Marie, her voice quiet, but with an intensity that brooked no argument. *The Guédé stood behind her, making violent gestures at the nurse.*

The nurse stepped back, panicked, sensing the unnatural ire. "Do it."

The nurse positioned the cart. "Stevens, call for a fetal monitor. Get Joe in to help."

Marie undid the gown. The girl's chest was motionless, a light alabaster.

"This is a waste," muttered the nurse.

"Hand me the defibrilators. Clear."

The body, shocked, lifted slightly off the bed.

Marie lowered her head, listening for a breath, feeling the arm for a pulse. "Clear."

"That was three hundred. Higher?" asked DuLac.

"I don't dare."

Marie massaged the heart. Nurse Jane affixed adhesive connectors. DuLac inserted an IV drip while Stevens gelled a fetal monitor to her abdomen. Joe drew blood.

If someone wanted to shout she's dead, he or she kept quiet. DuLac was an impressive figure. So, too, Detective Reneaux. But Marie looked both crazy and outraged, her arms and hands pushing hard against the chest, resting, then pushing hard again.

The monitor seemed to pick up a beat—elongated, ever so slow and faint.

"Malfunction?" asked the lead nurse.

Marie glared and kept working, ten minutes, twenty, thirty minutes. One by one, the nurses, the technician, Joe, drifted away to other patients, other duties.

The Guédé disappeared.

Reneaux was sitting on the visitor's chair, his elbows on his knees, his head bowed.

"Marie, stop."

"She's not dead."

"No, she's not," said DuLac, quietly. "But your treatment isn't working. Plan B, Marie. We need a Plan B."

Marie slumped against the wall. *Sounds mocked her: the respirator whooshing air, the occasional scratch, click, and whir from the monitors searching for signs of life. She could even hear the saline drip, racing through the girl's veins.*

She could try chemical stimulants. But how would they react with unknown drugs? She risked heart failure. Or some other side effect—an irreversible coma, lung, kidney, or possible immune failure. She wasn't in a lab dealing with test tubes, petri dishes, and disposable slides. Here was a young girl, a human being, a complex organism made more complex by an unknown drug.

"Don't get emotional." Think, Marie, think.

She opened her duffel bag, pulling out the journal. "It's here." She thumbed through pages. "The ingredients. Laveau asked how her husband Jacques became a zombie. Here. John's answer: 'The gills of a fish. Skull powder and grave dust. A simple spell. We sent all the way to Haiti.' Do you remember, DuLac?"

"*Oui.*"

"It all means something," Marie said, her voice straining, wiping away tears. "I can't figure out what it all means."

"Quadroon Balls," said Reneaux to DuLac. "We suspect old-time prostitution is being made new again."

"But the Quadroon Balls were meant to be more than that,"

insisted DuLac. "More like long-term mistresses. Second families. The children formed their own society, free coloreds who became doctors, lawyers, artists, educated tradesmen."

"You really think anyone today cares about paternity?" asked Reneaux. "It's murder without the family values."

"What about adoption?" asked Marie.

"One drop of black blood is still problematic," said Reneaux. "Catch-22. Who'd be the *aristos* of today? Rich white men. How many of them would want a bastard part-black child?"

"It doesn't make sense. Why not birth control?"

"Virgins. Innocents," said DuLac. "Men paid high prices for virgins. They wanted the deflowering. Wanted the girls finely reared like their white daughters. Wanted to educate them in carnal knowledge. Wanted to know that any child born was truly theirs. These were complex contractual agreements, 'shadow marriages.'"

"The *aristos* had the luxury of a pretend marriage, children to be proud of, and if they weren't proud of them or needed money, they could sell them into slavery like puppies. Or breed the boys to trades, the girls to become valuable mistress/whores like their mothers."

Marie held her patient's hand. "She probably thought she was just going to a ball."

"An escort service."

"But one that lasted until you got pregnant."

"Dead, undead is the punishment. Disappear the body, but even if it's discovered, no trace of murder."

"Technically, there *is* no murder," said Marie.

The three of them stood over the girl, mourning, as if at a wake.

"A pedophile's and rapist's dream," exhaled Reneaux. "Young girls playing dress-up. No notion of the terror to come."

Marie stroked the girl's hair. "Ah, *ma petite*."

"But why fodder for a steamship? Marie's right. Even though they appear dead, technically, there's no murder. There must be some other reason for the drug. Why risk actual murder?"

"*Oui*, Reneaux, why murder a girl off Riverwalk? Constant tourists. Casinos. Coast Guards. Lots of traffic in or near the Mississippi."

"Maybe she's the dare. The challenge."

"For who?"

"You, Marie. Maybe all along someone wanted you to find this girl? But it's not our secret assistant. It's the Devil, the perpetrator himself."

"Or herself," said Marie.

"Or both," said DuLac. "Male and female. They both sin. Voodoo and Catholicism agree."

Harsh hallway light flooded the room.

"What're you doing here, Reneaux? Helping your friend DuLac bury himself in waste? That's what you're doing here—wasting facilities, supplies, equipment." Severs, well dressed in a coat and tie, lacked his usual confidence. His hands fluttered like disoriented birds. He stuffed them in his suit pockets, looked at the girl cocooned in white sheets. "Looks dead to me."

"Are you a doctor?" Marie challenged.

"No. But neither are you. Not yet anyway."

"I am."

"Not for long, DuLac. Your alcoholism is plenty cause to fire you. Rescind your medical license."

"This is police business."

Severs flinched. "Trustee Allez is on his way over."

"How'd he hear?" asked Reneaux.

"This is media disaster. The trustees have been informed. Wasting money on a dead girl. Not even anyone important."

"How do you know that?" shouted Marie. "How do you know?" She was furious. "All girls are important."

"Not this one."

"You know who she is," said Reneaux, stepping forward. "'Media disaster' is a ruse."

"No," said Severs. "She's a type. Girls like her get in trouble. All the time. You can tell by looking at her."

"That's a nasty thought," said Reneaux. "I think you're lying."

"What do you mean by 'in trouble'?" demanded Marie. "'In trouble' because she's dead? Or 'in trouble' because she's pregnant?"

"Did someone tell you she was pregnant?" asked Reneaux.

Severs glared. His brow gleamed with sweat.

"You're lying," said Reneaux.

"Twenty-four hours," answered Severs. "Then, the morgue. I'll get a court order, if I have to."

"And I'll resign," said Marie.

"I'm not the one breaking the law."

"You sure?" asked Reneaux.

Severs puffed himself up, then flung open the door, his exit spoiled by the lack of sound. Rubber on the wall muted the contact between wood and metal.

"He's involved," said Reneaux, making a note on his pad. "I used to think he was harmless. My mistake."

Wearily, DuLac rubbed his eyes. "I need to get back downstairs."

"I'll stay," said Marie. "If ER can spare me."

"*Oui.* Take care of her."

"I will," Marie shouted after a dispirited DuLac.

"You want coffee?"

"Please. Black, Reneaux."

"Like me?" He kissed her hand. "I'm honest, unlike Severs."

"I like honest black men."

Reneaux grinned. "Great news, Doc. I mean, Doctor Levant."

"Just Marie."

"Okay, 'just Marie.' But you know you're more than that. You're not 'just' anything."

He gathered her in his arms, his hands rubbing her back, his mouth covering hers. Marie leaned into his embrace, letting herself take strength from his caress.

"I'll get you coffee, then I'm off. Want to get a background check on Severs."

"You promise to be careful?"

"Promise. Nothing will happen to me. I'll call Toxiology. Tell them about a paralyzing fish. I'll visit Breezy's, too. I think our insider is there."

"Jacques died there. He *was* dead, wasn't he?"

"You know he was."

"Strange. To think I'd rather he *be* dead, than be like her." She gestured toward the bed.

"It's not at all the same. You're going to save her. No one else will be buried alive."

"Promise?"

213

"Promise."

The door swung open, then closed. The room was dull again. Marie mourning for the girl.

Why did she feel so profoundly sad? For all she knew people were buried alive every day. Or shredded in a steamboat's wheel.

She'd been trained to accept grief. Every day people were eaten up by cancers; odd tumors bulged and grew. Epileptics fell to the ground with seizures. Cords bulged around an infant's throat. An immune system could attack rather than defend. A mosquito bite would itch one person, kill some other. Science didn't seem any more rational than the possibility of a hex or spell. Add in psychology, the power of suggestion, and anything could happen.

"There are more things in your heaven and earth, Horatio."

Marie wondered: Did Shakespeare learn of voodoo from the Moors?

* * *

It was just her and the girl.

DuLac was on duty; Reneaux, investigating Breezy's. Marie had faith Reneaux would find some answers. She had to find some, too. Some answers would take a lifetime of searching. Some demanded more immediacy. What sense was there to be a doctor if she couldn't heal? What sense to be connected to voodoo if she couldn't wield its power?

For the girl, time was running out. She was motionless, seemingly oblivious to senses. Smells, sounds, touch. *Did she dream?*

She looked like Sleeping Beauty except for the wires and tubes extending from her arms, chest, bladder, and mouth.

"You're not dead. You're not dead," Marie chanted like a mantra between the hushed whirs of machinery.

"Sure she is." Allez entered the room, smooth, dressed in an elegant tuxedo.

"When did you become a doctor?"

"Some facts are obvious, immediately verifiable."

"Severs has given us twenty-four hours."

"Did he now?"

Marie heard a light scratch. The girl's index finger moved once, twice. The nail lightly scratched the sheet.

Marie looked up at Allez. He'd heard it, and smiled, sardonically, as if he'd thrown down a gauntlet.

"You're evil."

"And you're not?"

The question caught her off-guard. Of course, she wasn't evil. She saved, not endangered lives. "You won't find what you're looking for here."

"How do you know what I'm looking for?" He moved forward.

"Don't touch her."

"So protective. Why? You don't know her."

"I'm a doctor."

"Your machines say she's dead."

Marie looked at the flat line, the lung machine expanding her ribs. She was a scientist. She wasn't supposed to ignore data and facts. She knew that. But her intuition counseled something else.

"It was you who C-sectioned Marie-Claire. You, who allowed another to be autopsied. Why spare this one? Or are you looking not to murder another one?"

"I haven't murdered anyone."

"So you say."

Marie swallowed a scream. She hadn't thought herself capable or culpable for murder. And, yet, there was the probability that Marie-Claire had been alive just as the girl on the bed was alive. She'd cut layers of flesh, delivered a baby and let a suffering mother bleed to death.

She reached for her purse, where the journal was safely hidden. She felt comfort holding Laveau's words close to her heart.

"So, you know who you be?"

Startled, she watched Allez step forward, seeming to drain the room's air. "You've found the journal I left for you."

"DuLac found it."

"I let him find it," he said, harshly. "I've been leaving clues for you all along. Didn't you sense it?"

"Did you leave her?" She pointed at the girl.

"No," said Allez. "She's a betrayal. As were the others. I prefer the swamp."

"So you're not all-knowing, invincible."

"Quiet." His hands gripped the railing; the bed skittered on its wheels. "Laveau was a formidable rival. You're an ignorant girl."

"You believe in voodoo?"

"No. But I want to believe. My father believed voodoo was good for business, and it was. It kept the weak in line. But I want to prove that the divine exists. I've heard the legends—Marie walking on water, possessed by Damballah, rescuing victims from fever, prophesying the future. The journal proves Marie's authenticity. Think, Marie. Think what it would mean to wield

arie stepped back, shocked. Surely, it was a reflex. Maybe a
her condition was improving? She was a doctor. "Heal."

arie leaned over the rail. *No dilation. No amber pupils
cting light.*

he leaned even closer.

*here was a world inside the girl's eyes. Images flickering like a
ie screen. Pictures from a grand ball. Dozens upon dozens of
-skinned girls, fans in their hands, dance cards dangling from
r arms—all giggling, twirling, locked in the arms of men.*

*Servants and musicians were black and brown men dressed for-
lly, yet stereotypically, with wide grins, white gloves, and shoes
king like taps. The male dancers were all white—some young,
st old; a few handsome, many well preserved. Some dragged on
ars, cigarettes; others sipped bourbon, brandy, assessing the girls
if they were cattle.*

*The scene was reminiscent of a mythic, genteel plantation—
asters bored with their wives searching for "harmless" fun; elder
tatesmen smugly believing young girls with even one drop of black
lood owed them their charms.*

*Beneath the atmosphere of alcohol, raucous laughter, and
ntense stares was decadence, evil, and lust for virginal girls. Even
the servants lacked conscience; all, except one. Marie recognized the
jockey man from Breezy's; he was leaning against a wall, his disgust
barely veiled.*

*Another picture: Allez and Marie-Claire, unimaginably
handsome together, linked arm in arm. Marie and Allez on a
balcony, overlooking a room decorated like Eve's garden. Then,
there were quick snatches of history: Allez and Marie-Claire
arguing; Marie-Claire slapping Allez; Marie-Claire running*

voodoo's power." Skin flushed, breath ragged, Allez appeared
crazed. Obsessed.

His timbre dropped lower; he spoke softly, intensely: "I want
to feel the spirits. Why else involve the DeLaCroixs? Now there's
you. All my life I've heard there was a Laveau descendant born
with a caul, with the possibility of real magic."

"You're looking at the wrong person."

"I don't think so. The DeLaCroixs keep track of their descendants. There was an eyewitness to your birth. Hands that buried
the caul."

"You're saying I'm related to the DeLaCroixs?"

"Your mother's birth name?"

"Cross."

He shrugged, his mouth twisted like a jester. "Of the cross.
DeLaCroix. Marie Levant née Cross, 1948–1980. After Laveau,
you were the first in four generations to have the caul."

"You knew Marie-Claire."

"Even in the biblical sense. She wasn't touched by the divine."

"That's why you killed her."

"No, Marie. You forget. You killed her. I've been told her child
was born with a caul. If you won't help me believe in voodoo,
then my child will."

Marie slumped forward onto her arms crisscrossed on the
bedrail. The world was unstable; the floor shifted like water; light
provided little clarity.

Allez, the baby's father. The baby, her cousin? Had she murdered another cousin, pulling life from her abdomen?

"Don't set yourself against me, Marie. I have money. Influence. It makes much better sense for you to join me."

"Join me." Those were John's words to Marie Laveau. *Join him in corruption, undermining spirituality. In the end, Laveau had to kill him.*

Allez's face twisted. He was ugly, pursuing his passion. His hands shook the bedrail. "Don't . . . set yourself . . . against me."

Head up, Marie answered, "I will. I do."

"Do you want to end up like her? Like Marie-Claire? Like your mother?"

"What do you know about my mother?"

His shadow elongated, draping the girl's body, trailing halfway up the wall. "I only have to say a word or lift my hand, nod my head and you'll be wiped off the face of the earth. Twenty-four hours won't do you any good."

Marie studied the girl's delicate hand, the slender fingers, translucent skin and blunt nails painted pink.

All the possibilities for a girl hadn't changed—there were always men who believed that being men gave them the right to seduce, overpower, and harm. Beware to any good woman or man who tried to stop them.

Her mother had spent her entire life hiding from a man. Allez's father? Then Allez? Marie knew there was no gain, no peace to living in fear.

Allez was weak. She must remember that. Why else would a grown man need to control innocents? He was insane, too. Intent on the divine when his soul lacked grace.

She had to be cunning. Use his pride against him. Her guilt, too. Allez was right. There was blood on her hands.

She hadn't understood that the young women were still alive. One thing she understood from Laveau was that hatred was

more effective turned outward than in.
rect, but it could ease the burden on one
Christians turned the other cheek. Vood
the Old Testament, encouraging the n
defending those unable to defend themselv
the Old and the New. Just as voodoo marr

Marie had no idea what she could do
were—she only knew she had to try to save
as many women as she could.

She thought of all the harm and hurt this
mother, lungs struggling for air. Fury made h
landscape. Her mother hid; she'd take the
should have taken. As a doctor, she warne
become too emotional; as a *voodooienne*, she'd
refine it to a blazing heat.

She looked up at Allez—a big man filling a
with a deadened heart.

She said softly, scornfully: "Don't you know
die?"

Allez's anger was palpable, his face taut. His f
the girl's pillow, barely missing her face. He'd kill h
without conscience.

Abruptly, Allez turned. "Twenty-four hours." The
wildly on its hinge.

"Mon piti bébé. Fais dodo." Marie caressed the girl's c
mother is worried about you. Let's get you home. Te
going to be a grandmother."

The girl opened her eyes.

down the stairs. Marie-Claire lying dead, undead in a weeping woman's arms.

The image changed. Violin bows falling and rising in three-quarter time. The room was a whirl of silk, lace, and satin. Girls floated in a sea of pastels. Men, in funeral black, their backs ramrod straight, spun and twirled the girls to slaughter.

To the far right was a staircase. A golden-haired gentleman, a small paunch protruding over a cummerbund, escorted a petite brunette upstairs. Fifteen? Sixteen? The girl wanted to keep dancing. But the man tugged, relentless: one hand, pushing against her waist; the other, pulling her right arm.

Was this the future?

The eyes closed.

"No, wait. Please."

Eyelids fluttered, reopened.

The brunette girl was screaming, being dragged toward an altar. Allez tied her arms behind her back. A woman's hands, nails bloody red, put something in the girl's mouth; then pinched the girl's nose and covered her mouth.

Dead. Undead.

"Where?"

The image panned outward. A three-storied mansion glowered white. Vines and moss strangled the columns and lattice trim. Huge willows, their branches hanging like teardrops, shrouded the east and west sides. The yellow moon was sliver-thin in a midnight sky.

Surrounding the house was bayou—marshy swamp, sluggish streams, inlets of blackish water covered with velvet moss. Overgrown, riotous trees grew out of earth and water. Thick underbrush and timber cast shadows where predators hid, crawled, slithered, and walked.

A woman with gold-hoop earrings, her hair wrapped in a red chignon, stood on the porch. Her hand upraised.

Marie saw a mirror of herself, older, her brow and mouth lines etched with deep lines.

"Dare you," the woman seemed to say. "Dare you."

A hoot owl screeched, sweeping up its prey without mercy.

NEVER ENDING

Two Thousand and Five

When the screaming began, no one, except Marie, had seen Marianne.

She looked like an aristo, *though the guard who hurried her along called her "Negress"; "Nigger"; "Whore." The guards waited for darkness before touching her.*

Acts committed wordlessly—grunts, explosive breathing, terrified screams.

How many? Three, four, five? aggressive men laying claim to a delicate girl.

Marianne survived three nights.

—Marie Laveau speaking to Louis DeLavier

She ran down the steps to the ER. "DuLac. Allez is behind this." DuLac was stripping his gloves and medical
coat, cleaning up after an asthmatic attack.

"There's another Quadroon Ball. Or there's going to be."

"You don't know?"

"No. I only know I have to be there. Allez's mad."

"Someone will be hurt?"

"Yes. I've got to stop him."

"Marie. Wait for the police."

But she was already dashing, heading for the automatic doors.
Barking, Kind Dog scooted up from beneath Sully's chair.

"Stay, Kind Dog. Stay. Call Reneaux, Sully." Doors slid
open. There was a whoosh of humid air. A smell of sulfur and
smog.

DuLac shouted, "Marie!"

Her keys in her hands, she jogged left toward her car. There was a bark, then Kind Dog leaping past her, across the driver's seat, onto the passenger seat.

"No. You've got to go."

Kind Dog cocked his head. Licked his bandage.

"You've hurt yourself." Marie hugged him, stroking the length of his spine. "I don't want anything to happen to you."

Kind Dog, patiently, let himself be held, then scooted face forward.

"All right, then. Let's go. But you'd better stay safe."

* * *

Marie had made this journey before. To Teché, bayou of snakes. From the journal, she now knew this had been Marie's childhood home. But Marie and her Grandmére had lived in a stilt shack. Not an antebellum mansion.

Nonetheless, Marie knew she was part of this world. The landscape resonated in her soul. Teché. Home of the DeLaCroixs. Kind Dog's old home. Baby Marie's, too. She had an affinity for this world. An affinity built on fear, old ghosts, and newly discovered ancestors.

Every mile that drew her closer, she wanted to turn and motor back to the city. The landscape had frightened her once. Now she'd have to face the sights and sounds again, the menace that went bump in the night.

The highway gave way to dirt trails. The road was jarring; ruts made her spine shake and Kind Dog whimper. The overgrowth and trees became denser, highway light more remote. Fewer and fewer cars. Until none. Just the loneliness of a darkened road. Headlights capturing creatures scampering, owls diving for prey, bats gliding through air.

The air conditioner struggling with humidity, the Beetle's

wheels moved ten miles per hour. The moon played peek-a-boo and shadows elongated then disappeared.

She felt eyes were hidden in the trees. Someone—*something*—was watching her.

No one should be out on this forgotten road if they didn't have to be.

She stopped at the roadside where she'd hit Dog, where her Beetle had been turned belly-up.

Sitting in the car, she and Dog, both panting, watching mist caught in the car beams, Marie couldn't helping thinking "primeval." How foolish she'd been not to wait for Reneaux. Did she think she could drive farther up the driveway and walk right in? And even if Allez's men let her pass, what was she supposed to do? Demand they give up the girl?

Her head touched the steering wheel.

Her door was yanked open; startled, she screamed. Reneaux placed his hand over her mouth. "Sssh. Don't you know you're supposed to lock the doors?"

"You scared me."

"I didn't mean to. Besides, Kind Dog saw me. Move over."

Kind Dog stepped gingerly to the back; Marie moved over to the passenger side. Reneaux slipped behind the wheel.

"I didn't hear your car."

"Parked a ways back." He quickly kissed her. "You look tired, Doc. Not your usual composed self. You seen a ghost?"

"Are you trying to rile me?"

"You bet," he drawled. "I'd rather you be mad at me than feeling bad."

Marie hugged him, holding tightly, passionately.

"It's all right."

She wiped tears from her eyes. "Sure it is. Did you bring more police?"

"Chief didn't believe me. Said no sense fighting crime that hadn't happened. Or was a woman's overwrought imagination."

"It isn't my imagination."

"I know. Voodoo—mystical. Unexplainable."

"You don't believe me?"

"I do. But it *is* mystical. Unexplainable." He turned off the headlights; the gnats and mosquitoes caught in the beams disappeared. The darkness was blanketing, thick.

"I have my own score to settle with Allez," said Reneaux. "His father murdered my brother. Not directly, but without a doubt."

"Is this what you tried to tell me?"

"Confession's good for the soul."

"I can't absolve you."

"I didn't think you could. But I wanted—still want you to know everything about me."

Marie inhaled. She couldn't see Reneaux's eyes, mouth. Only the cross glinting in his ear.

"Simple tale really. Sold crack. Thought helping my mother justified the crime. One Sunday, I was late with deliveries, sleeping off a hangover with a girl whose name I didn't even know.

"Thirteen, Jean decided to help." Reneaux stopped. Marie heard him pounding his fist into his thigh, beating back the pain.

"He was sweet, my little brother. Liked reading mysteries. Chester Himes. Raymond Chandler.

"He got robbed, his throat slit. An addict, one of my best

clients—a hyped-up petty thief, never remembered the killing. Adding insult, Allez's father wanted his lost profit. It was his dope I was dealing.

"I was on the run for a while. Came back as a cop."

"I'm sorry." Marie and Reneaux both stared out into the darkness. Insects lighted on the glass. Kind Dog lay down on the backseat.

"I dream about my brother. I wake up in sweats, seeing his flesh, the blade."

Marie laid her head on his shoulder. "It haunts me that Marie-Claire might've felt pain."

"She would've wanted you to save her child."

"But at such cost."

"Maybe she called out, reached you with her mind."

"Do you think?"

"Why not?" he said, his breath warming the darkness. "All I know is it's not your fault. It's Allez's fault. The DeLaCroixs' fault. Both families have seeded the world with drugs, gambling, prostitution. Both DeLaCroixs—the mother and grandmother were responsible for their daughter and great-grandchild. You've done more than either of them."

Reneaux reached inside his jacket. "Enough confessions, let's concentrate on stopping them. Do you know how to use a gun?"

"No."

"Here." Reneaux clicked on the interior light.

The gun was sleek, shiny black. In her mind's eye, the gun's barrel was draining blood. "I fix gun damage. Not cause it."

"There's no one else here but you and me."

Reluctant, Marie took the gun.

231

"The cartridge clicks in here. Here's a spare. Put it in your pocket. Once the cartridge is snapped in, release the safety, aim, then shoot.

"Remember. We don't have a search warrant. If it's just a ball—escort services—prostitution—we should come back. We have to see someone inflict harm."

"I had another vision. Saw a girl dead, undead."

"Then a rescue. In and out. No one seeing. Agreed?"

"Agreed."

Reneaux shut off the light and the engine.

* * *

Reneaux clicked on his flashlight. "Let's go."

Marie turned on her light. Kind Dog was beside her.

Reneaux flashed the beam of light down a narrow gravel trail. "Invited guests go this way. Spoilers," he directed his beam into the woods, "the back way. Ready?"

Marie nodded. They slid down the embankment, onto wild ground. The soil was soft; sluggish water flowed above and deep beneath the surface. Mud sucked at their shoes, inching up their ankles, their pants. Mosquitoes, gnats, ticks were searching for exposed skin. Reneaux slapped at his throat; Marie pinched a blood-sucking tick from her wrist.

There was a flurry of sound. A small animal—rabbit? squirrel? rat?—squealed before dying. She and Reneaux trudged deeper into the untamed land. The universe was darker. Marie focused on the sound of Reneaux's footsteps, pressing and releasing mud.

Willow, cypress, and oak strained high, arching into a canopy of green, blocking out the moon and stars. Vines fell like curtains, stroking skin, feeling like tentacles, cobwebs. Ferns slapped against arms and legs.

There was a sharp embankment. Reneaux shouted, "Careful." Then slipped, and in a second, he was up to his waist in swamp. Marie threw him a vine, thick as a snake, and pulled him out. An animal splashed into the water.

Reneaux murmured, "Crocodile."

Marie shuddered. The land was a perfect defense. One main road. No surprises for the guards. A man or a woman could get lost. Probably starve or be eaten.

"Why not dump the girls' bodies here?"

"Allez says they did."

"Except for the last one. A calling card for you."

"No. Allez says he didn't do it. Maybe it's our helper. Maybe the girl was never intended to be tossed overboard."

"Another clue."

"Yes. Just more desperate than the others." Marie stumbled. She couldn't help envisioning bones decomposing in the swamp.

Kind Dog limped badly. Mud oozed into his bandage.

Marie guided him to a tree base, patted the ground. "Stay. Kind Dog. Stay." She rubbed his ears, whispering, "Be safe."

Dog whimpered, pacing back and forth like a caged lion.

"He'll settle down," said Reneaux, his beam shining north. "Let's keep going."

Marie looked back. Dog was watching her.

* * *

Buoyant, high-pitched, violin strains contrasted with the untamed earth, the dark water packed with leeches, eels, and water moccasins.

233

Things unseen disturbed Marie most. Tormented spirits. Not *loas* like the Guédé. But souls who'd lost their lives too early; souls who'd experienced suffering, abuse. The closer she came to the house, the more she felt the spirits. *Recent and old—generations of history. Thousands of souls aching, all tied to a plantation house, now controlled by descendants of ex-slaves.*

"Keep low," said Reneaux.

The house rose like an illuminated white monster, rows upon rows of windows lit with candelabras. A fountain with white, baby-faced cherubs gurgled and sprayed foamy water. Greek columns spanned the wrap-around porch.

Dozens of sedans and limousines were parked in the driveway. Chauffeurs lounged while guards patrolled the porch and perimeter.

"Heavy artillery," said Reneaux. "AK rifles. Machine guns. This isn't a tea party," he drawled. "No ordinary southern hospitality."

Marie said nothing. There was a foulness in the air. She wanted to blend back into the night, the overgrown swamp land. But a girl might die. Or worse. Become undead.

They inched farther up the embankment.

The first floor had mammoth French doors and bay windows. There was a clear view of couples whirling, waltzing like this was nothing more than a grand cotillion. Men bowed low; girls curtsied. Bodies merged and flowed in stately, intricate measures.

"It's a 'who's who' of Orleans' underworld. Most of them scum, bottom dwellers, cruel enough not even to want to pretend respectability. Except here. Dressed like overstuffed penguins.

"Drug lords, casino kings, interstate fences who move a million a day, some skinheads, liars, tax cheats, murderers. My, my," said Reneaux. "Twenty-first-century good ole boys."

"Look there."

"Severs. Shit. And Logan, another hospital trustee. He's a police captain. And see the one with the thick mustache? He owns a luxury hotel in the Quarter. What do you know? Outright criminals and the gutless ones who hide behind respectability."

The antebellum South come to life. With twists: overseers and masters. As if there'd been no emancipation. It was a grinning minstrel show but far more elegant and deadly. Quadroon girls, bubbly with champagne, were being offered to the highest bidder.

"Is this how far we've come?" Marie murmured. "Folks still wanting to believe in the white superiority myth of the South."

"Power. Segregation and race-mixing controlled by a black man."

"And Madame DeLaCroix?"

"According to city records, she owns the house. Ssssh."

A guard walked straight toward Marie and Reneaux, belly-flat in the wet soil. Marie felt some creature crawling up her pants leg.

The guard stared into the woods. If he stepped an inch to the right, looked down, he would surely see them.

"What is it?" shouted one of the guards.

"An animal, I think." He lit a cigarette, inhaled, and blew rings of smoke. "Time for a drink soon."

"Snatch. Time for some snatch, I think." One of the guards chuckled; another hollered, "Black and brown snatch for the likes of us." A voice called, "Be alert," and the men quickly quieted.

Reneaux, crouching, moved toward the back of the house. Marie followed. There was a clearing marked by stones and pans of beans and rice. An altar was covered with multicolored glasses of burning candles, knives, even a machete. Buried in the altar's heart was an iron rod, another crossed it, a third up from the bottom.

"Upside-down cross," Marie whispered. Wrapped over the intersecting joints was a snake. Maybe a moccasin. Or a boa constrictor. "Alive?" she asked.

"Don't know. Allez's unique evil. Blasphemous and exotic."

"Voodoo as Devil–worship."

Marie saw the Guédé, their hands reaching skyward in lamentation. The smallest Guédé mimed dancing, then eating and falling across the altar.

"The girls were drugged here," she said, her voice reed-thin. "The wind carried their screams, dispersing them into the air."

The second Guédé danced, pretended to swallow and fall down dead. The third and tallest Guédé mimed unzipping his pants; then, grotesquely, he feigned sex with the other Guédé. Flopping them on their knees, their sides, running, without tiring, between the two.

"Most times, it was one girl, occasionally two. Once drugged, the men abused them."

Marie buried her face in her hands.

"How do you know this, Marie?"

"The Guédé. They're trying to stop the outrage." She looked, transfixed, toward the altar. *A cacophony and calliope of girls: some wailing silently, some beating the earth, some immobile with fear. Women from three centuries, fighting for their lives, sharing a common fear.*

"Can you go on, Marie?"

She stared blankly, then fixed on Reneaux, matching her breaths to his. "Yes."

"There's a servants' staircase off the kitchen." Reneaux hooted, throwing his voice to the west. "Southern boy trick. Next time go." He hooted again and Marie curved left, then upward to the right. Slipping through a side door, she could overhear the cook complaining about not enough greens and pâté. A waiter howled, "Not enough champagne." A scullery boy was slapped, then told, "Hush," when he started crying. "You lazy boy."

Heart racing, Marie tiptoed up the stairs. *Coming down the stairs was a ghost; a house slave from long ago who carried a tray of café au lait and half-eaten toast.* At each creak, Marie pressed her back and hands against the wall—terrified some servant or guard would discover her. *The house ghosts seemed to move about their business, centuries old, acknowledging Marie with a grim smile.*

The house was maddening. *Two worlds: past and present. Both mannered and decadent.*

Lilting music and laughter drifted up the stairs, a sharp contrast to the somber sounds on the second floor. *She heard whispers punctuated by soft cries.* On the landing, she saw a man dragging a girl down the long hallway decorated with elaborate scones and white molding. She could barely move. *Haints, ghosts were lingering in torment. Some, their faces to the wall; others, milling about aimlessly.*

A child needed her.

Marie moved quickly down the hall. The man opened a double door and pushed the girl in. She stopped before the door, her hands touching the stained wood.

Where was Reneaux?

She didn't hear anything behind the door. Old wood usually talked, but from behind this door, she heard nothing.

She could stay outside the door and be caught or go in. She clicked off the gun's safety and stepped inside a suite decorated like an Egyptian revival harem.

There was a room on the left. She could see an ornate satin bed, hear whimpering, see black-panted legs shifting, slightly lifting and sinking deeper into the mattress.

She held the gun steady. The girl, her dress hitched up to her thighs, silk stockings and garters showing, was being crushed into the mattress. Pounded hard.

Marie cocked the gun. The man lifted himself off and over the girl, his face red and perspiring, his penis flaccid. The girl, crying, smoothed down her dress and covered her breasts. The white satin was stained red.

Marie kept her gun fixed on the man. No tenderness for a woman believed to be disposable. Still, the girl was alive; she was the brunette of Marie's vision.

"Come with me." The girl's streaked eyeliner and mascara made her look younger. "Get up. I'll help you."

"She wants to stay here." The man grabbed the girl's arm.

"Let her go." Reneaux's gun was trained on the man's heart. "Sorry I'm late."

"You're here when I needed you."

Marie reached for the girl. "Let me help. I'm a doctor." She helped the girl walk, feeling her ribcage shuddering, her lungs gulping, fighting for air.

In the hall, Reneaux lifted the terrified girl. She cried against his shoulder.

"Let's hurry, Marie."

"Something's not right." She paused, arrested by a smell—a chemical, man-made, not organic smell. Or was it the reverse? *Some unfamiliar, organic smell. Primeval. Latent in the darkness. She'd smelled it at Breezy's. Heavy and rank. She heard screams and whispers, indistinguishable words. The house was trying to share secrets.*

At a door, the Guédé were waving her in.

"In and out, Marie. We've got to get this girl out of here."

"Reneaux, please, wait." She was drawn to the door. *Each step she wanted to undo, but the Guédé waved her on, encouraging.* She stopped at the door.

Her hand touched the brass knob.

She opened it and almost screamed. Rows, like a girl's dormitory, of sleeping beauties. All of them dead, undead. *The stink settled in her hair, her clothes. Sounds were raised to a fever pitch.* Marie clamped her hands over her ears.

The girl in Reneaux's arms screamed, hysterical. "Home. Please take me home."

"What's your name?" asked Reneaux.

"Sondra."

"Sondra, we'll get you out of here. But stay calm."

"Marie," insisted Reneaux, tugging her. "In and out. We've got our witness. We'll come back for these girls."

Her eyes red, Marie mourned, "Too late."

Allez and two other men stood behind Reneaux.

"I've been expecting you."

Reneaux set Sondra down. A guard frisked him, took his gun, a switchblade from his pocket. Leaning against the hall wall was Sondra's rapist—his pants up, shirt loose, fly undone.

"Take her," said Allez. The drunken man lurched, fondled Sondra's breasts, then dragged her down the hall.

"Help me," the girl screamed.

Marie cursed; Allez blocked her path. The second guard pressed a gun to Reneaux's abdomen.

"Let her go."

Allez laughed. "Marie, the optimist."

"Then let Reneaux go."

"To spread ugly rumors about our parties? Impossible. An honest policeman is a liability, a risk." Allez nodded at the guard. The guard fired his gun.

Reneaux's expression was stunned surprise. Holding his abdomen, he fell backward, as if a rope was tugging him down. Nothing to cushion his fall. Fall, falling down flat.

Sound was trapped in Marie's throat. She could see the bullet's course, flying through flesh, abdominal muscle, into intestines and stomach. No blood spread outward from Reneaux's back. The bullet was lodged inside.

She dropped down beside Reneaux. His mouth was gaping, his chest rising and falling rapidly.

"Let me see." She lifted his bloodied fingers and saw the gaping hole. A .45 hole, with sulfur, gunpowder, cotton fibers, and ragged flesh. "Call an ambulance."

Allez crouched. "The only person who can save him is you, Doctor Levant. Maman Marie. He's your only patient. Use voodoo or medicine, whatever you like." Allez rose, motioning his guard to leave first. "I'll be back in an hour. Either he'll be dead or you'll have saved him."

"What do you want from me?"

"A miracle. I want to know if you can save him."

"You're crazy."

"Pass the test and I'll promise not to murder those you love."

"There isn't anybody."

"Reneaux, of course, will probably die. As Jacques did. Did you know Jacques was a friend to both you and Marie-Claire? And what about DuLac? El? No love for them? What about Marie-Clarie's child?"

"You were at Breezy's."

Allez smiled. "I'm everywhere. This world and the next. Heal him if you can, Marie. You're running out of time."

* * *

Reneaux was in shock. He needed to be kept warm, the bleeding stanched. She stole a pillow and sheets from the girls' beds. "I'm sorry," she said. The girls kept sleeping like princesses. Except it was the deranged prince, not the witch, who cast the hateful spell.

Reneaux's blood was soaking into the wood. She knew she couldn't stop the bleeding. She had nothing to operate with—no scalpel, no sutures. He was dying. His life's blood slowly draining.

Downstairs, folks were dancing. The music and chatter masking sounds. Allez was probably even now bartering another girl for money.

"Reneaux, can you hear me?"

His tongue wet his lips. Marie bent close. His lips touched her ear.

"Out of here," he mumbled.

"I'm not leaving without you."

"Out." Exhausted, he coughed. Blood was draining into his lungs.

Hell. There wasn't any way to save him. All the tools she needed were in an ER van or at a hospital. Cross-legged, she sat on the floor, frustrated and crying.

"Marie, child"—the words echoed from the walls. "Marie, child."

The Guédé were sitting cross-legged, across from her, next to Reneaux. Close-up, she could see their skeletal faces and sunken eyes.

"Marie." The sound wasn't from the Guédé. It was a woman's voice. Faint and plaintive.

"Marie, child, she could touch a child's brow, and lift the sickness right up into her hand. Once a man near death, chest aching, lungs choking on fluid, called for the Virgin, but it was 'She who Worships the Old and the New' who told him, 'Hush, go to sleep,' and when he woke, his fever was gone, his lungs clear."

"Mother?"

"They called her Queen. Queen of the Voodoos. Marie Laveau."

"Mother, please."

She felt a chill in the air, then a rush of warm air, circling her, making her feel safe. She inhaled, a mist flew inside her mouth. It wasn't her mother. It was the other Marie.

Marie felt an intense love.

"You are my child. Women hand sight down through the generations. Mother to daughter."

Marie felt both powerful and vulnerable. More woman than she'd ever felt.

"Not all the Maries could carry the load. Some corrupted by the New World; some controlled by base men. Some had their scores to settle. It was I who killed my daughter's father. How could she ever forgive me?

"You are my child, too. Believe. Learn and believe."

"I will."

Marie felt a great peace, then felt Marie leaving. "Don't go. Save Reneaux, please."

"It's in your hands, Marie. In your hands."

Reneaux's body shook, reflexes and connections misfiring. A spot of blood drained from his mouth.

The Guédé began drumming, their hands beating upon their thighs.

It's in her hands. What did that mean?

She pressed her cheek to Reneaux's. "I could've loved you."

That wasn't true. She did love him. Burgeoning, not fully grown; yet love.

She imagined Reneaux whole. Upright, faithful, and strong.

His cross earring rested on the side of his neck. Reneaux believed in Christianity, in voodoo. He believed in her.

She feathered his face with kisses. Her lips pressed against his black skin, rich like the night sky, reminiscent of African warriors.

Everyone was mixed blood. He was her good ole southern boy, and she loved him . . . loved how he teased her out of her ill humors . . . how he cared about goodness, justice.

She touched his head, his neck, his chest, arms, and thighs. She touched his wound, feeling his warm blood between her fingers. His breath was getting shallower.

She laid her hands atop his hands, pressuring his abdomen . . . holding what life remained, in. *She focused on loving him . . . loving her mother . . . the newborn, Marie . . . a circle of love, powerful and strong. Her hands clutched his—the blood sluggish and bubbling. "Heal," she whispered, feeling pain, heat in her hands. Her mind imagined science readily available . . . sutures, antiseptic, scalpels, bandages, and stapling gun. Her mind imagined miracles.*

"Heal."

Blood slowed, then stopped. Reversing its course, the bullet moved backward from the spine, through muscles, sinews, and surface skin. Reneaux's arms relaxed, his hands fell to his sides. He opened his eyes.

"Marie."

"You're not out of the woods yet."

She stared at her hands, as if she was one of those faith healers on late-night TV. The Guédé were gone. The Sleeping Beauties ever calm.

Reneaux gripped her hand. "I love you."

"Rest, if you can. I've got to find a phone. Get help."

"Thanks, Doc."

"Marie." She kissed his brow, touched her cheek to his. "I'll get help."

"No help coming," said a voice. "Out here, everybody is on her own."

A panel in the wall had opened, and a woman in a white blouse and rainbow skirt stood framed, a candle in her hand. There were warrens behind the walls; there was a rush of stale air as the woman walked forward. Marie clasped her hand over her mouth. The closer she got, the more the woman appeared to be Marie's mother come to life, resurrected from the dead.

The woman kneeled, examining Reneaux's wound. The dulling red, the caked blood, the torn flesh regaining color. "You're a healer," she said, awed. "Not a charlatan like me."

"You're Marie-Claire's mother?"

"Your aunt, too. Sister to your Maman."

"I don't believe you." But she did. Allez hadn't lied; she could see the same bone, hair, and coloring imprint—the brown skin, the eyes set wide, black hair. More interesting than beautiful.

"My face mirrors yours. Mirrored your Maman's, too."

"Then help us," begged Reneaux.

"*Non*. The Laveau family split long ago. Some kept the name; others changed to DeLaCroix. Laveau's daughter was alive when jazz was being born, when folks feared voodoo more than they do now. Marie's daughter thought it humorous. Why not reinforce devil worshiping? Walking with zombies? Christianity, like the cross, turned upside down? What better revenge on her mother? Marie Laveau, so self-righteous. The daughter incarcerated her mother, then promoted herself as her mother reborn."

"How cruel."

"No less cruel than Laveau killing her daughter's father."

"John deserved to die."

Madame DeLaCroix shrugged. "So the story says. What does it matter? All daughters meant to trouble their mothers. If your Maman had lived, you would've troubled her, too."

"Not true."

"Certain?"

Marie said nothing.

"You might've despised her weakness. Didn't you grow sick of hiding?"

"Don't listen to her, Marie."

"My mother was good."

"Bah. Your Maman didn't believe voodoo should be a business. Your Maman was a fool."

"Don't say that."

"'Tis true. She was my sister. I knew her well enough. Children together, she'd cry over every little thing. A fly caught in a spider's web. A flower trampled. Some boy tease her and off she run. Hide in a corner, face to the wall."

"Stop it."

"She didn't have the strength to be a Laveau. Or a DeLaCroix. Levant, so mundane, barely a pseudonym at all. Do I look my age, girl?"

Marie was unnerved by the change in subject.

"*Non*. Much to be said for roots, herbs. Even creating the

undead, nothing but knowing a recipe. But I wasn't born with a caul. Hasn't been a descendant for over sixty years that had the gift. You did. That's why your mother ran."

"I'm glad she ran."

"Liar. The family needed a child touched with the divine. Think who you could've been."

"You're not my blood."

"All things alive. Snakes are stirring in our blood. You healed him, *non?*" Madame let her fingers brush Reneaux's chest. "You're a true descendant."

Madame rose, her fists balled, nails digging into her flesh.

"Marie, we've got to get out of here." Reneaux struggled upward; Marie helped him rise, her arm about his waist.

Madame drew close, her voice softly venomous. "I bet you did more mothering than your Maman ever did."

Marie was a child again, her mother home from house cleaning, physically and spiritually exhausted. She'd rub her feet, brush her hair, fix a cup of tea and rice. Her mother never said: "Go out and play"; "How was school?"

Buried deep was her guilt, her wishing for another mother. Her mother—always so intent on hiding, hadn't even succeeded in that. Yet she'd done her best. Marie was only now beginning to understand that.

"How do you think black people survive in this world?" said Madame, rising, towering over Marie and Reneaux. "By being strong. Crafty and courageous. No evil we do compares to what was done to us."

"Is that why you're with Allez?" asked Reneaux. "To intimidate? Do more evil?"

"Ah, the policeman. What has your goodness done? Kept your brother alive?"

"What has your evil done?" hissed Marie. "Kept your daughter alive?"

Madame shrilled, "I could turn you into a snake. Make your blood thin. Hex you for a thousand years. Send your soul to the Devil."

Marie stood and faced her aunt. She could see traces of her mother, herself, Marie-Claire. Without a doubt, Marie-Claire's daughter was in danger. Marie looked at her hands. Looked at Reneaux, worry creasing his face. Looked at the Sleeping Beauties harmed by her family. Her mother had done the best she could. Loved her as best she knew how. She searched her heart. Allez was right. The DeLaCroixs were her people. She saw the sweat on her aunt's brow. How her nails damaged her hands. And she knew that, in her own way, her aunt was weak, too.

"I can choose. Isn't that the point? Laveau's descendents chose to do good or evil, to be charlatans or healers." This was the revelation.

She stepped closer to her aunt. "You're a witch. Your threats are only good for the powerless, the weak. I won't be intimidated. *Je suis Marie.* My gifts are real."

"You can't frighten me." But Marie knew she did.

"If you had any real power," said Reneaux, "you wouldn't be with Allez."

"I've done well with Allez's father. Built an empire. Made a fortune."

"Too bad Allez thinks to replace you with me."

"Who are you to talk?" Madame demanded. "You're nothing.

Just as my sister was nothing."

"You murdered her," said Reneaux, solving a piece of the puzzle.

"You did, didn't you?" murmured Marie, startled by the depth of evil.

"Jealousy," said Reneaux. "Look at her face, Marie."

For the first time in her life, Marie wished she weren't a doctor. Wished she could murder as easily as any criminal.

"Why?"

"She had you."

"She was your family. Your sister. Your blood."

"I'm a woman of unnatural feelings," Madame answered bluntly.

"Your daughter? You made her undead."

There was a flicker of pain; Madame's nails dug into Marie's arm. "That was Allez."

"But you knew about it. You encouraged the rape—"

"It wasn't rape. Marie-Claire loved him."

"Seduction of a minor is rape by law," said Reneaux.

"You knew Allez would tire of her, drug her . . ."

Then her eyes, face hardened like Medusa. "I am a woman of unnatural feelings," she repeated. "A Voodoo Queen."

Where her mother was soft, Madame was hard, where her mother was weak, Madame was strong. What would it have been like to have had her aunt as her mother? They would've survived Chicago—no poverty or embarrassment. No loneliness or being outcast. Her mother had been ineffectual in all but her goodness.

As if she could read her thoughts, Madame said quietly, matter-of-factly, "If you'd been my daughter—we would've ruled the world."

Marie winced. But she understood. Goodness was the essential quality. Like honeysuckle, it was ephemeral, beautiful—but fortifying. Her mother had chosen to live her life as a sleepwalking beauty, a kind of undead, to protect her daughter. She'd done it out of love.

Marie studied her aunt. Hardness made her less human.

Her mother was imperfect. Vulnerable. Just like Reneaux. Just as she was.

"I am Marie. My mother's daughter. The true line of Voodoo Queens."

Her aunt twisted with rage, a skull luminous beneath her skin; she'd die, worms eating her flesh. History . . . time forgetting her.

"Why not me?" screeched her aunt. "Why not me and my daughter?"

Marie felt hard, unforgiving pity.

* * *

"My, my a family reunion." Allez sauntered into the room. "Not dead yet?"

Madame plucked at threads in her skirt. A guard trained his gun on Marie. Reneaux stood tall like the brave cop he was.

"A miracle." Allez walked a circle about Reneaux. "You've been resurrected, I see. Amazing." His fingers touched where the bullet had entered, where blood still soaked Reneaux's shirt. "The divine is real. If it helped you, it should help me."

"Turn yourself in, Allez," said Reneaux.

"Amazing. I never would've believed— Better than your aunt's mumbo jumbo, half-hearted spells. Marie, you are a true descendant."

"Go to hell."

Allez cackled with glee. "Don't you understand? With your powers, my influence, we'll prove to the world voodoo is real. Authentic power."

"I won't help you."

Allez turned to Madame. "So much more than your paltry powers. A miracle. Are things ready for the ceremony? Tonight will be exceptional. Let's get our faith healer downstairs."

"Allez," said Madame. "You can't depend upon her. She'll betray you."

"And you haven't? Never has a *loa* touched you. Never have you answered my prayers for the divine."

The guard pulled Marie toward the door. Reneaux knocked the gun out of his hand. The man shoved Reneaux, sending him tumbling to the floor.

Allez grabbed Marie.

"I don't belong to you," she screamed.

"You will." Allez squeezed her jaw in his hand. "You'll do what I say to keep Marie-Clarie's baby safe."

"My grandchild? What has she to do with this?"

Marie looked at Allez, suddenly comprehending. "Didn't Allez tell you? Your granddaughter was born with a caul."

"You didn't tell me."

"Our blood is alive, not his. Do something."

"Shut up," said Allez.

"You didn't tell me," railed Madame.

"You're better than him."

"He's a criminal," said Reneaux.

"Take her," shouted Allez.

251

"You won't make me help you," screamed Marie. The guard lunged for her again. Reneaux's fist cracked the man's jaw.

Allez took a gun from his pocket. "Let me show you how I can make you. No second miracle allowed." Gunpowder exploded. Reneaux's chest spurted blood.

Reneaux looked disbelievingly at the wound. Another shot. His head snapped up and back. Blood drained, down the rim between his eyes.

"You didn't tell me," Madame moaned.

The world washed red. Marie fainted.

* * *

She woke—lying on a bed in a row of beds filled with Sleeping Beauties, dressed in shifts, covered with white sheets. At first, she thought she was dead, undead. But when she whimpered, sound tickled out of her mouth.

"Awake?"

Allez, legs crossed, was sitting relaxed in a chair, a perfect picture of western sophistication. A double-breasted suit. Cuff links; a gold and diamond ring on his finger.

"Why?"

"Because I could. Because all my life I've been trying to prove miracles."

Reneaux was lying on the floor, a sheet casually tossed over him. Blood stained the floor, the top and middle of the sheet.

Marie swallowed bile, wanting to understand more than she wanted to forget.

"And the girls? These young women?"

"A hobby. Prostitution has always been profitable."

"Why not let them have their babies?"

"Like kittens. Too many. Who needs another black single mother?"

She wanted to spit, rail at him. But she'd one more question.

"Why dead, undead?"

"It was the spell closest to a miracle. Or should I say, closest to the appearance of a miracle? When your aunt explained it, I knew others would be awestruck. Power—controlling someone's life is addictive." He leaned forward, his finger drawing a spiral on Marie's arm.

"Besides," he said offhandedly, "you'd be surprised how exciting passivity can be. Knowing you can do anything you want without objection. Knowing there's a mind alive, inside the body, heightens the ecstasy."

Marie attacked him, flailing like a witch, her nails drawing blood, tearing at his shirt. Her suddenness had caught him off guard. But it took only seconds before his arms were bending hers behind her back, before the weight of him was pushing her down onto the bed.

He was breathing hard. Pinioning her arms, flattening his weight on her until she couldn't move.

He was aroused; her body went limp, still. She didn't know whether he'd attempt rape. Straddling her, his lids half-closed, Allez kissed her throat, the hollow between her breasts.

"Did you enjoy Jacques?"

She didn't move.

"From the moment your plane landed in New Orleans, I knew everything about you."

"You killed him."

His hands roamed, delving beneath her waistband, touching the hairs of her crotch.

"Coincidence. Jacques knew Marie-Claire. They'd been schoolmates. He wanted her to leave me. Oh, he didn't know it was me. Just knew, Marie-Claire was under the influence of a bad man." His breathing labored, he continued groping, pinching her breasts and buttocks. His mouth and tongue left half-moon marks on her throat. "An interesting irony, don't you think? Sleeping with your cousin's friend. Heh, *Chérie?*"

She sank her teeth into his shoulder. Allez hit her; she saw a thousand stars.

Life be a celebration. Being a woman be just fine.

—Membe, Marie's African ancestor

She was outside, on a pallet, tied down, her mouth still tasting of blood. Stars and moon were overhead. Kind Dog was licking her face. "How'd you get here?"

She touched her face to his, feeling his cool nose, smelling his damp fur. He looked terrible, covered in burrs and mud; she wondered if his leg would need to be reset.

A voodoo ceremony was in progress. The altar was on her right. On her left was Madame DeLaCroix, sitting stoically as if she were waiting for tea to be served—as if ceremonies to sacrifice young girls were as natural as breathing.

Allez was wearing white pants and a white jacket over his bare chest. He looked like an island pimp. He lit bowls of rum, the flames rising like magic. Sighs from the crowd; the men discarded their jackets and shoes. Some tore off their shirts, their flesh rolling like waves over their belts. Others hooted and hollered like monstrous schoolboys. Servants kept refilling cups of rum. With each beat of the drum, inhibitions faded. With each beat, the men became more primitive.

Severs was on the far right, the light-bright man observing for the least resistance. But none of the bearded or gray-haired men had the maturity to stop obscenity.

Good men like Reneaux and Jacques died. These men were pillagers, rapists.

On the porch, young women dressed in their ballroom finery were herded like so many cattle, eyes glittering—some with fear, others with excitement; some seduced by champagne, the temptation of spectacle; still others looking for an escape, wanting to go home from a party gone bad, from a party where real men held real guns.

Marie catalogued her injuries: bruises on her face, a cut lip, sore ribs. Nothing life-threatening. The hardiest pain was in her heart, but she couldn't think about Reneaux now. She had to save herself, the young women, and Kind Dog. Dog, who licked her face, who'd walked miles through a swamp to save her.

The drums shifted beats; the syncopation was sharper, faster. Allez waved a torch like a banner: "Dance," he shouted. "Time to dance."

On cue, black and brown women, topless, skirts slit up their thighs, darted forward, dipping and swaying suggestively. Some of the men darted forward to stroke the dancers; others joined the dance, reveling like participants in a bacchanal; still others masturbated without shame. The quadroon girls cowered; many cried; guards surrounded them.

Voodoo—the bestial, the black exotic. Voodoo—the barbaric, exhibitionism without the spiritual.

Marie cursed in frustration. She didn't understand everything about voodoo, but she knew it wasn't this; if she survived, she'd spend her life letting black people, all people, know that voodoo was loving and good, not hurtful and evil.

A cage of squawking chickens sensed their doom.

"More rum," shouted Allez. "More rum."

Allez was king. He slapped his palms against his chest. "See me. See me. I am the king. *Le roi.* King of the Voodoos. King of the Zombies."

"Eh, yé, yé, Allez," the crowd chanted. "Eh, yé, yé."

He strutted, accepting his due. Envious, men slapped his back; some bowed low without mockery or shame. Others kissed his ring as if he were a bishop or king.

Marie struggled to sit upright. Women would be dying soon. That was Allez's notion of voodoo.

Madame DeLaCroix remained still, unnaturally composed.

Marie looked at the altar, the upside-down cross. The snake, wide as a man's strong arm, was curled about metal.

Allez chanted:

> Legba, Legba, remove the barrier for me
> So I may pass through
> Legba, remove the barrier
> So I may pass through to the spirit world.

But there weren't any spirits. Instead, a drummer, like a pied piper, led two light-skinned women dressed in virginal white out from the mansion and down the porch steps. Their eyes were unnaturally bright. Marie suspected they were drugged. At

DuLac's, spirits had come; here, compliant women descended into a pit.

The drumming was intricate, louder:

> Legba, remove the barrier
> Remove the barrier
> So I may pass through to the spirit world.

Allez's body seemed to tremble. "The gods have come."

But that was a lie. Marie didn't see, feel, or hear any spirits. Allez was playacting.

Men yelped and screeched. Some pretended possession; some heralded gods they didn't believe in; most acted licentious just for the pleasure of it.

Women kept dancing, their skirts twirling, exposing naked buttocks and thighs.

"I am king. King of the Voodoos. King of the Zombies." Allez was the perfect showman. *"Roi de la Voudon."* He slit a chicken's throat, wiping blood on his chest.

He turned toward the altar. "Damballah, enter me. Come."

Marie knew no miracle would happen. The ceremony had all the reality of a carny show: cheap thrills and tricks. Any minute now they'd bring out the two-headed man or the midget alien. Except Allez and his followers maimed, killed. Real damage was inflicted by their illusions and parlor tricks.

The bonfire, the drums, the blasphemous altar, even the humidity thickening the air, lacing flesh with sweat, added to the atmosphere of mystery and power. Fireflies danced like crazed lanterns.

Eh, yé, yé, Madame Marie
Marie makes zombies
Eh, yé, yé, Madame Marie.

Madame DeLaCroix looked so much like her mother it was eerie. Looked like Marie would look thirty years from now. Still lean, angular; high cheekbones.

Her mother had worn her hair in a neat twist; DeLaCroix wore her hair long and wild like a mantle.

If Marie thought hard enough, she might feel sorry for Madame—doing so much harm, so alienated from her family. But tonight, seeing her step forward, seeing her kiss Allez, seeing her swaying her hips, taunting the men as though she was twenty not sixty, Marie felt revulsion.

The drummers kept pounding, calling the gods.

Allez raised Madame's hand high. "*Le roi.* The king. And this is my queen."

Madame began shrieking, flicking a fan as if she were possessed by Goddess Ezili. Ezili, Mary, and Mary Magdalene suggested in one spirit.

Next, Madame picked up a sword, flashing Ogun's blade at the roaring crowd. Even Severs seemed transported.

Allez was before her, on his knees, "See, see, Marie. With you here, we're touching the divine."

Marie spoke slowly, carefully. "This is a lie. All of it."

"Madame—"

"—is pretending. As you are."

"Call the gods, Marie. Call them for me." He stank of sweat, rum, and compelling fear. He desperately needed, wanted to believe.

Marie looked beyond Allez. Sondra was being dragged down the stairs. Her hair was tangled, half upswept, half dangling with pins. Blood was on the front of her dress, her chenille ripped.

Kind Dog howled, his howl blending with the young women's wails. Sound spiraling up to the moon, into the wildness where no one would hear. No attempt at rescue.

The two young women in the pit clutched themselves as Sondra was thrown in to join them. A valley of hell before the altar.

"Call the gods."

"I'll have nothing to do with you."

"Damn you," muttered Allez, before leaping into the pit, gathering Sondra in his arms, lifting her high as his sacrificial offering.

Marie struggled against her ropes.

Something made her look up toward the window. The jockey man, the one who spoke to her at Breezy's, was watching her. He expected her to do something.

What?

Surely she could do something with all her hatred, her rage. Hatred for the careless disrespect of human life. Rage that a mother could be such a monster. That Allez could make voodoo a farce.

Her hands were tied, literally. Why couldn't she say abracadabra? Make the world better?

Kind Dog, looking up at the window, wagged his tail. Had the jockey man been the insider, the one to leave clues? He raised his hand, almost like a salute, and Marie nearly cried.

Why did he believe in her?

She closed her eyes. Have faith. She could hear DuLac's voice, clear and distinct: *"Call the gods."*

Marie flexed her fingers, trying to increase circulation. Kind Dog licked her hands, tried to unloose the knotted rope.

> Eh, yé, yé, Madame Marie
> Eh, yé, yé, Madame Marie
> Makes spells, makes zombies.

Allez set Sondra down before the crowd of men. Terrified beyond screaming, she tried to crawl away in the dirt. Men on either side of her reached out to touch her hands, her dress, her shoulders, her hair. Legs formed bars.

"*Call the gods, Marie.*"

A circle had formed about Sondra. Allez was shouting, encouraging the men to "Believe. Miracles happen." The dancers swayed, the men pushed forward, their hands scrambling, straining to see. DeLaCroix joined the chant:

> Eh, yé, yé, Madame Marie
> Makes spells, makes zombies.
> Eh, yé, yé, Madame Marie.

Marie was frantic. How could she save anyone? "Call the gods, Marie." She closed her eyes. "Don't be emotional." *Call the gods.*

She whispered: "Guédé."

And she felt them—coolly moving inside her—soft as silk, cold as ice, darker than the bayou on a moonless night.

"Guédé, have mercy."

These were the spirits she'd dreamed about . . . these were the spirits who'd entered her during her dreams, and when she stopped dreaming of them, they haunted her footsteps, guiding her, encouraging her to discover the undead.

"Guédé, Guédé, have mercy, don't let me lose my way."

Sondra stood before the altar, two guards holding her reverently, beneath her elbows and palms as befitted an offering. The girl, no longer struggling, was resigned to her fate. Severs lasciviously stroked her hair. The other two girls stood behind them like bridesmaids, gun barrels touching the small of their backs.

Allez was roaring, "Voodoo makes miracles. Voodoo makes spells."

Madame was mixing herbs with a mortar and pestle. Making a batch of poison to mimic death.

Marie looked up again at the house's windows. *Ancestors, spirits, fragile women in ball gowns, female slaves in coarse cotton, some in undergarments, some naked and ashamed—young women, old women, middle-aged women—all who'd been under the brunt of some man's thumb—peered down into the yard, their mouths puckering like fish out of water.*

Break the bonds.

She saw Death's Kingdom, a shadowy world paralleling the living. The mansion was filled with ghosts. Haints. Spirits bridging the world between the living and the dead. Bones rose from the bayou and the mansion was soaked in blood, a setting for misery and murder.

Break the bonds. She was the link between worlds, between faiths.

All along the Guédé had been resentful.

Marie stepped forward, the Guédé strong within her. Kind Dog was barking crazily. Her arms had the strength of ten men. She pushed men aside and kept on her path toward Allez, Madame, and Sondra.

"Voodoo makes miracles. Voodoo makes spells." With her fist, she felled Allez. Men rushed forward, and she shouted, "Leave him be. It's a test of his faith."

The crowd fell back, because Marie, herself, seemed ten feet tall. Her voice resonated with three voices—ancient Guédé who sang the sound of a terrible death.

A guard fired a gun. Marie raised her hand, folding her fingers over metal and gunpowder. The guard stumbled backward, dropping his gun. Several more guards abandoned their posts.

The crowd was mesmerized, watching a miracle, watching Marie, the Voodoo Queen. All their lives they'd seen brutality, even caused it; never had they witnessed such a rift between good and evil. A glimpse of powers beyond their world.

Madame held on to Sondra as if she were a shield.

"It isn't time for her to die," said the Guédé/Marie. "Your time is coming soon."

Madame blanched.

Allez struggled to his feet.

"Look," said Guédé/Marie, her voice resonant with disaster.

Everyone looked upward. Fire spontaneously lit the mansion's curtains. One by one, the windows, the multitude of eyes were alight. The women spirits were at work.

Drummers stopped drumming; men screamed; dancers and young girls ran into the bayou.

Allez shouted, "Water."

"Stay," said Guédé/Marie, and Allez couldn't move, his limbs paralyzed, his body held tight by a Guédé.

Madame DeLaCroix pleaded, "Mercy."

Fury bubbling inside, the Guédé/Marie spoke, "You'll traverse the world without end. Ever lonely. Ever undead, dead without end."

Madame let Sondra go. Prostrate on the ground, she cried, "Mercy."

"Run," said the Guédé/Marie to Sondra. "Hide."

The two girls in white, intended as Sondra's sacrificial companions, wailed, restless, confused.

The Guédé/Marie blew kisses. "Run. Hide."

Marie lifted her arms skyward and wide. She exhaled and the second Guédé flew out of her mouth. He moved with grace, efficiency. He moved, touching a lock of hair, a shoulder, a leg, a hand. He caressed a man's face. Any and all that he touched fell down dead.

Men were screaming, scurrying from the demon they couldn't see. Flames were licking the roof, running down vines, leaping across trellis, slats, and dry moss. The air was acrid, smoke-filled, cackling as sparks wafted high.

The snake on the cross uncoiled, inching down onto the altar.

DeLaCroix made the sign of the cross. "Hail, Mary, full of grace, the Lord is with thee."

Marie and Madame; niece and aunt. Family yet enemies.

The Guédé/Marie clasped Madame's throat and squeezed. Marie's hands felt gloved, encased in cotton—she couldn't feel her aunt's flesh, the blood pulsing through veins. Madame flailed, a scream trapped in her throat. The Guédé's hands tightened.

"No, Marie." It was Reneaux, his voice like a gust of wind. "Leave it to the police."

The Guédé pressed with renewed vigor. Madame would die.

"No, Marie. Don't let this happen. You'd never forgive yourself. Choose."

Choose. Yes, she could choose.

"Guédé, go."

The Guédé-loas flew out of her mouth. Madame fell, gasping.

"Reneaux!" Marie searched, but he was gone. Disappeared like the Guédé. Without a trace, without a sound, no breeze echoing her lover's voice.

The house was burning out of control. Heat washed over her; black and red smoke reached the clouds. People scurried like rats in a maze, trapped by fire, smoke, and swamp. The Sleeping Beauties were dying. Marie dried her tears.

The snake was curled on the altar—thick, gray skin with specks of yellow coiled like a never-ending spiral. Marie stroked it. It was cool; its mouth yawned.

"Damballah, are you there?"

Allez's kingdom had fallen. Bodies twisted in the dirt. Grown men beat the ground crying. One man was on his knees, hands clasped in prayer. Women huddled, their dresses bathed in gray flecks of smoke, burning particles of wood. Car engines roared as drivers left their masters; some intrepid souls ran into the swamp, preferring their chances in crocodile-infested waters. Only one man stood his ground—the jockey man, his lips pressed into a grotesque smile.

Kind Dog barked. Allez was coming toward her.

"You don't frighten me."

"You frighten me. You, with all your outrageous powers. You, touched by the divine."

Marie laughed, hearing the hysteria in her voice.

Allez was serious. He was no longer the arrogant spoiler. Or the criminal who hurt without forethought or afterthought. His coldness and power had been stripped away. He was a supplicant.

"Join me," she said.

"I will. I do."

"I require a test of your faith."

"Yes," he said, unmindful of the fire, the danger, eager like a novitiate to prove his worth. "Yes, Maman Marie."

"Maman Marie," echoed Madame DeLaCroix, rocking, her arms wrapped about her abdomen. "I never meant to hurt my daughter. Allez convinced me. I never knew she was pregnant. Never knew she bore a child with a caul."

"It was my seed that made the miracle." Allez slapped his chest, shouting fiercely. "My seed. Maman Marie, we could reshape the world."

Marie was sickened. She picked up the snake. It was beautiful, strong. In the firelight, its skin reflected rainbows. She murmured, "Damballah, are you there?"

Long, long ago, Marie Laveau set a snake against John.

She held the snake's head close to her mouth, whispering, "Damballah, if I'm really yours, really your priestess, then take Allez. Make justice right in this world."

She offered the snake to Allez. "Take it, Allez. I won't force you."

"I know this story. Your namesake murdered John this way."

"Marie never murdered him."

"You're saying John lacked faith. That's why he died, isn't it?"

268

She said nothing.

Skin damp, breathing harsh and uneven, he spoke urgently, "John never believed in the divine."

"Do you believe?"

"I've been searching all my life." He held open his arms.

Damballah slid from her arms to his.

What was it Laveau had said? "Because of what you did to me, to Maman, Grandmère." None of it had changed. Two centuries. The same scene of vengeance was being played out.

Her soul hurt. Her mother was dead; her grandmother was an old woman who'd cowered before her daughter, afraid to save a grandchild or great-grandchild who needed love and care.

Hysteria threatened. "Don't get emotional."

The snake hung like a rope in Allez's arms, its tail and head dragging in the dirt; then, as if on cue, the snake blinked, lifted its head, and curled up Allez's arm, traversing his chest.

"Allez makes miracles. Allez makes spells." He was spellbound, watching the snake, feeling it slither, curling about his body.

Madame was moaning, "Have mercy, have mercy. Hail, Mary, full of grace."

The snake squeezed . . . and squeezed. Slowly, inexorably, as Allez waited for the divine, waited for the gods to bless him, his flesh tightening, his muscles bruised, his ribcage straining, ready to crack.

Marie turned her back on him. The jockey man saluted, and Marie understood that he'd been the insider, using the undead girls' bodies as clues. Should she thank him? Or challenge him for not having enough courage to call the police, to save the girls outright? But what did she know of his motives, the frailties that might've hampered him?

Severs stood over Allez's body (his legs twisted awkwardly, his eyes popped wide). Far away, almost like a dream, sirens wailed.

"End of a career," Severs mumbled. He looked at her. "I could tell you why I did it, how I was seduced, trapped."

"I don't want to hear."

Madame crawled forward in the dirt. "He's dead."

"It's over," said Severs.

"He's dead," Madame repeated.

"A test of his faith."

"You'll murder me, too."

"No," Marie answered. She crouched beside her. "You're not a daughter, not my mother's sister . . . not my aunt . . . nor grandmother to your grandchild. You're nothing in this world."

The Guédé appeared, nodding, in unison, their hats in their hands.

"I see them. I see them."

"Your miracle at last."

"My miracle at last." She clutched Marie's hand. "This is what my granddaughter will see?"

"Most likely more." There were a host of *loas,* not just Guédé, black-faced gentlemen guarding death.

"One of my descendants with sight."

"There are no more DeLaCroixs. Only the one bloodline, down through the generations of Laveaus. Blood will out. *Le sang se manifestera,*" insisted Marie. "*Comprenez-tu?* One family, one name."

"*Oui. J'comprends.*"

270

"Bon. Je suis Marie."

"What will happen to me?"

"What do you think should happen to you?"

Sirens loudly complained; tires crunched on gravel. DuLac must've persuaded the police to send help.

Marie stood.

"I didn't intend to kill her. Just make her undead."

"Death would've been preferable." Kind Dog rubbed against Marie's leg. "You'll never be forgiven. Even if you die of natural causes, you'll wander for eternity without a home."

Madame DeLaCroix inhaled and gracefully rose. The burning plantation house was her backdrop.

"Marie," DuLac called.

Police yelled, "Stand down. Stand down." Gunshots sounded. DuLac moved forward, a policeman, gun drawn, at his side.

Severs raised his hands in submission.

Madame smiled ruefully: "I'm a Voodoo Queen. A woman of unnatural feelings."

Marie watched as her aunt glided toward the altar, watched as she calmly drained her potion, watched as she collapsed like a marionette doll.

"Eh, yé, yé, Mademoiselle Marie," said the jockey man, startling Marie, his mouth close to her ear. "Madame has always been a bad one. She used to steal your mother's dolls. Cut their plastic necks."

"Comment t'appelles-tu?"

Policeman handcuffed, chased after worshipers. Severs looked small and insignificant.

"You'll find out soon enough. Take care of your cousin. The

great-grandchild." Nimble and fleet, he moved to the back of the altar and into the wild.

The Guédé clapped their hands.

Kind Dog barked.

"You can see them, can't you, boy?"

Glass shattered, exploding outward, floorboards collapsed, a great billow of smoke rose over the bayou.

"Marie." DuLac stepped forward, embracing her.

"Reneaux's dead."

"Ah, *ma petite*. He was a good man."

Another explosion. The staircase crumbled, came shuddering down.

"Every goodbye ain't gone," said DuLac.

"I know. His ashes are in that house but his spirit is everywhere."

"So you understand."

"A little. One step at a time."

"Women hand sight down through the generations. Mother to daughter."

Marie nodded. "Let's find my child."

Kind Dog limped badly. DuLac supported an unsteady Marie. *The moon glowed red. The three Guédé walked behind them.*

Marie looked over her shoulder. *The Guédé blew kisses. Behind them, women chattered, laughing gaily, as if they were in a parade. The plantation house was a burning wood-frame skeleton. A centuries-old cycle had ended. Spirits and secrets were set free in smoke. A quadroon girl—Laveau's Marianne?—curtsied deeply, her hand pressed to her heart.*

"Let's go home," said DuLac. "El's worried sick."

She smelled honeysuckle. Somewhere in the wave of spirits was her mother. She stopped, searching the joyous crowd of ghosts.

"See. I told you. You have the sight."

"You don't see them?"

"*Non.* I leave all miracles to you. Your heart's big enough."

"You think so?"

"I know so."

Kind Dog barked twice.

Marie echoed the words: "Heart big enough . . . like my Maman. Like my daughter will have."

As the spirits danced away into the distance, Marie's heart overflowed with love, with Christian and Voodoo charity.

She knew where she belonged: in Charity Hospital—her hospital—carrying on the faith.

"Come on, Kind Dog, let's go home."

any New Orleans residents claim that Marie Laveau lies in a tomb in St. Louis Cemetery No. 1, where to this day the faithful bring offerings and prayers. In St. Louis Cemetery No. 2 there is a crypt covered with crosses scratched in red brick by followers who believe Marie rests there. Others claim that Marie Laveau never did die.

Author's Note

I always planned to write a sequel to my first novel, *Voodoo Dreams*. *Voodoo Dreams* has a special place in my heart, because the novel helped me grow up and taught me, like Marie Laveau, to appreciate truly the glory and wonder of being a woman: powerful; spiritual; in control of her life and body; valuing ancestors, family, and community.

Voodoo Season is the first novel in a contemporary trilogy in which Marie Laveau's descendant grows stronger and also more vulnerable.

What's the sense of living if we don't open our hearts to love . . . accept our imperfections and recognize that life is a journey, never ending? Our spirits never die . . . and each of us has a responsibility to leave a legacy of grace, kindness, and mentoring to our children and the next generation.

Read *Voodoo Dreams,* the novel that started the journey; enjoy *Voodoo Season;* and look for Marie, healing and loving, in the next novel of the trilogy, *Voodoo Jazz.*

LAKE COUNTY PUBLIC LIBRARY

3 3113 02379 9648

Lake County Friends of Public Library

X RHOD
Rhodes, Jewell Parker.
Voodoo season

LAKE COUNTY PUBLIC LIBRARY
INDIANA

AD	FF	MU
AV	GR	NC
BO	HI	SJ
CL	HO	CNL OCT 05
DS	LS	

Some materials may be renewable by phone or in person if there are
no reserves or fines due.   www.lakeco.lib.in.us   LCP#0390